# IT STARTED WITH A GIGGLE

On a night out in Edinburgh, single mum Liza-Belle Graham finds herself revealing her hopes and dreams to a green-eyed stranger. Liza has always wanted to run an 'arty-crafty-booky' business, and she's seen the perfect empty shop ... But Scott McCreadie is an interior designer looking for new premises. And when Liza arranges a viewing she bumps into none other than Scott trying to steal her perfect shop! Is Liza's dream in jeopardy, or is a new dream about to begin?

# KIRSTY FERRY

◆

# IT STARTED WITH A GIGGLE

*Complete and Unabridged*

# LINFORD
Leicester

First published in Great Britain in 2020 by
Choc Lit Limited
Surrey

First Linford Edition
published 2021
by arrangement with
Choc Lit Limited
Surrey

A catalogue record for this book is available
from the British Library.

ISBN 978–1–4448–4684–3

Published by
Ulverscroft Limited
Anstey, Leicestershire

Set by Words & Graphics Ltd.
Anstey, Leicestershire
Printed and bound in Great Britain by
TJ Books Ltd., Padstow, Cornwall

This book is printed on acid-free paper

# Dedication

*To everyone who dreams big — you can do it! (Schubert says so.)*

# Acknowledgements

I loved writing this book about Scott and Liza, and of course Schubert the Cat. It is, as you will know if you are a Schubert fan, the third in Schubert's series of books about a madly mystical family and their various love lives. Scott is the eldest McCreadie sibling, and he roared into my imagination on his motorbike one day, dismounted, folded his arms and tapped his foot until I agreed to write about him. Liza was the perfect partner for him, and of course ten-year-old Isabel is a law unto herself. I was a ten-year old girl and I have had a ten-year-old child — granted he's a boy, but he had ten-year-old female friends, and we are still close to those girls and their families today. A lot of their wonderful confidence and dramatics went into making Isa come alive and she's one of my favourite characters.

And 'Phoenix Antiques' is a real place. Well — it *was* a real place, and indeed the building still stands on the corner of a row of terraces near Crawcrook, in Tyne and Wear, complete with the panelled windows which may or may not be very similar to the 'Books, Paintings, Antiques' windows in Liza's shop. It's been an empty shell for as long as I can remember, and I always promised myself I'd write about it. The inside, as I describe it in the book, is based very much on a similar place near where my mother-in-law used to live. So comfortable was she in the tea shop one day, that she dozed off over her carrot cake and they didn't have the heart to wake her up!

To help bring all this to life and set Schubert off on his latest waddle through the literary landscape, I must thank my fabulous editor, wonderful cover designer and the whole Choc Lit 'family' I must also thank the splendid Panel (Megan C, Stephanie H, Isabelle D, Karen M, Linda S, Hilary B, Joy S,

Alma H and Cordy S) for agreeing we could let Schubert loose again, and the Stars who helped choose this brilliant cover. It makes me smile every time I see it! Thanks also to my family who tolerated my wittering about the book and who will (hopefully) feed me prosecco and/or gin and/or chocolate to celebrate publication. And a huge 'mow wow' from the star of the book as well, to all his loyal fans out there!

# 1

## Liza

It's my first night out in God knows when, and to be honest I don't even think I'd be here if it wasn't that my boss was retiring. His name is Auberon Bunbury, and I always think that's a hysterical surname for a vet, but of course I've never said anything.

'Come out with us, Liza!' Magda had begged. 'You *never* come out.' Magda is Eastern European and she can't quite get the fact that my name rhymes with 'Tizer', rather than sounding like a more traditional 'Lisa', but she does her best.

However, my ten-year-old daughter, Isabel, is having a sleepover with her best friend and mortal enemy, Sophie, and I'm enjoying myself immensely. We're in quite a fun sort of pub just off

1

the Royal Mile, in Edinburgh, and I'm loving the nineties music that's blasting across the bar. I've always had a soft spot for that dance music, even if it was popular way before I was a teenager myself.

Tonight, part of me isn't the thirty-one year old sensible working mum; it's the twenty-year-old wild child who danced on tables and could drink anyone under that very table, before suggesting a crowd of us should head back to our student flat for cocktails. In my mind, I'm way back in my youth and the music and the atmosphere is making me remember who I was and what I was before I had Isa. It's also, ironically, making me remember what dreams I'd had and what I'd shelved in order to bring up this little tiny ball of fury that has consumed me for the last decade. I love her more than I ever thought it possible to love someone else, but it's certainly not always been easy on my own.

Tonight, though, I've only had a

2

couple of glasses of wine and I'm already pretty tipsy — which clearly means I'm a lightweight now — and, as I'm staggering to the bar for my next drink, I do the classic 'Sozzled Liza' manoeuvre of tripping over something. Tonight, it's a chair leg.

A hand comes out of nowhere and steadies me and a little *zing* shoots up my arm and I giggle, all embarrassed now, because I'm not *quite* as brazen and fearless as I was ten years ago. 'Sorry! Sorry about that — whoopsadaisy. Wine. You know. Hee hee.'

I stop myself before I sound too maniacal, and the owner of the hand, a man, laughs. 'That's fine. I'm pretty sure it was the chair leg that was at fault.'

A memory stirs somewhere of someone saying a similar thing to me, but the wine is making my mind a wee bit hazy and I push the memory away as my cheeks burn up with a sudden mortification, and I think I need to sit down, actually, because the room's going all spinny . . . 'It was. It was *deferably* at fault,' I mutter, and he's still holding my hand and he leans across and gets hold of my other hand and I get a whiff of his aftershave, which is woodsmoke and spice, and my legs go a little more wobbly.

'Come on.' He guides me gently into the chair that attacked me, and there's amusement in his voice. 'I'd buy you a drink, but maybe you'd be happier just sitting here for a bit?'

'Aye.' I nod decisively. 'I would. But *then* I'll have a drink.'

'Great. I'll be happy with you sitting here too. And then I think *I'll* have a drink as well.'

I find that desperately amusing for some reason and giggle again, and we start a sort of conversation.

As we chat, I realise that this guy is really a lot of fun, and as my eyes start to focus better, I see that he is also very good-looking. Another three chaps are ranged around the table, and they all look a bit like him, only I don't think they're *quite* as good-looking.

'Excuse my brothers,' this guy says. 'They just called in for half an hour.' He looks pointedly at his watch and then looks pointedly at his brothers. 'And I think that half hour's up now, chaps.'

But it's as if we are sitting in our own little bubble here, and the nineties' music seems to fade into the distance as I giggle again and nod and the brothers grumble and grouse and melt away, leaving me and the stranger together — as well as some of their unfinished drinks. 'They're my younger brothers,' he says, looking at them, half-smiling but also watching as if he's making sure they are definitely leaving us. I know this, because I can't stop watching him watching them because he's completely arrested my attention. 'They're better now they're grown up, but still.' He turns to me and there's a devastatingly gorgeous smile on his face, and I kind of catch my breath a little and blink stupidly at him. Green eyes and a drop-dead gorgeous smile. The memories start doing cartwheels in my already woozy head and I know that's a dangerous combination under any circumstances — but especially when a person — particularly a person like me — is a little tipsy.

Before I know it, we're leaning into each other like we've known each other for years, and he's telling me all about his work and it sounds amazing — apparently he's an interior designer. I can't take my gaze away from his lovely green eyes, even though one of them is covered by a thick, floppy fringe of dark hair. I've always had a thing for green eyes, and I'm instantly attracted to these ones, although green eyes have led me into a world of hurt before now. I batter the feelings down as something is definitely nagging at me and making me remember things I don't really want to remember, and making me go even hotter as certain things come back to haunt me.

But despite all that, I can't seem to

stop talking about my hopes and my dreams, and he's making me want to tell him things I haven't really told anyone before, especially when he goes into more detail about his interior design business.

'I started out working for someone else,' he says, 'in a picture framer's and home accessories place. And then I realised I liked to spend more time planning the displays and choosing frames and mounts for the pictures than my boss really liked, and I didn't really like taking orders from anyone. Eventually, I lost my temper with it and with him, and walked out. I got another job, but in that job, I was *still* being told what to do. So I did it again — and again and again. Until I realised that the only thing that would stop me being dictated to, was if I was my own boss.

'I decided to branch out on my own and *really* design stuff — put my own stamp on it, kind of thing. I tried fashion design, and that didn't work out, but I still wanted to create — and there's just something so special about creating something for someone, and taking ownership of that design; and you know they're going to love it, because it's been done with them in mind. It's sort of magic, the way it all comes together.' He wiggles his fingers like a magician and winks. 'Listen — Freddie Mercury agrees.' He holds up one of those wiggly fingers as Freddie's famous and similarly named song echoes around the bar and I find that hysterical for some reason.

'They were playing the nineties' stuff before!' I say, mock-indignant. 'When did we go back in time?'

'I was distracted. I don't know.' He grins at me and those green eyes twinkle, and I press my knees together and hope he doesn't notice my jaw dropping with the sheer beauty of those eyes drilling into my own. Then he holds my gaze for a second, before his face flickers and clouds for a second. 'Aye.' He suddenly seems a little deflated and looks at the table, frowning. 'Some things in life you wish you'd pursued a bit more — but fashion design and working for other people aren't those sort of things. For me, anyway.' He frowns again and looks back up. 'Not at all. But how about you? Anything you wish *you'd* done differently? Anything you'd really go back in time for?'

*So, so much!* I want to say. But hey, I've only just met him, so I find myself confiding in him about something quite neutral, but close to my heart anyway. 'I'd love to open up a little gift shop. Like an arty-crafty-booky shop. You know?'

'I know.' A bottle of wine that I didn't notice before has somehow appeared on the table, and he fills two glasses. 'So you'd like your own business too?'

'I would. In fact, there's an empty shop on Methven Street. Bay windows.' The floodgates have opened, and I find myself spilling it all out to this green-eyed stranger. 'On a corner. Lovely place. Used to be Phoenix

Antiques, I think, if you look at the sign. It's up for lease. I pass it all the time.'

'Really?'

'Really. Of course, I'll never do anything about it, but it's nice to dream.' I sigh and turn my glass around by the stem. 'Sometimes, I think I should just grab my dreams and go for it.'

'Sometimes,' he replies, those eyes drilling into mine again and stirring up, briefly, stuff I thought I'd buried eleven years ago, 'you should just do what feels right, *when* it feels right.'

I blink and nod. It's a bit cryptic, but I get it. I've done that before . . . oooooh, about eleven years ago maybe . . . and it's not always the sensible option.

'The thing is,' I tell him, 'it's not always the sensible option.'

He laughs and empties the bottle of wine into our glasses. 'Sometimes, it's nice not to be sensible.'

I giggle and pick up my glass.

10

'Sometimes. And sometimes, well, it works out in some ways, I think. To the future, then.' I raise the glass in a mock toast. 'Where I've grabbed my dreams and I'm a proper businesswoman.'

He starts to go a little blurry around the edges, and I realise I'm way beyond my new, and pathetic, capacity for drink. Despite that, I drain my glass and stand up, a little unsteadily. 'I should go. It's past my bedtime and I'm drunk, and I should probably say bye-sie bye to Auberon Bunbury because they're all over there some- where.' I flail my arms wildly in the direction of my work colleagues. Aub- eron is three sheets to the wind himself, but I only know that because he's smiling soppily into the middle distance and has photographs ranged out on the table before him. The pictures are probably his collection of Labradors. 'One of each colour,' I mutter. 'One. Of. Each.'

'Whatever you say. And good luck with those dreams.' The green-eyed stranger raises his glass in return. 'It was nice to meet you.'

I laugh, taking in his lovely dark hair, his sparkly eyes and his dark clothing. 'And you,' I reply.

I wander across to my friends and say goodbye, then totter off to get a taxi back home; back to reality and back to my daughter.

It would have been nice, I think, if I'd got his name.

## Scott

The red-headed girl from the bar is right. I've always had a lot of time for red-heads, and this one was the most interesting one — and prettiest one, if not the drunkest one — I've seen in a long time.

I grin ruefully to myself and stamp the memories of pretty red-heads from my past down, back where they came from. I shake my head. Lost dreams aren't ones you can chase. Time to focus on current and future dreams . . .

And here I am now. On Methven Street. How very peculiar and entirely unexpected that I should find myself here . . . And there is indeed an empty shop on the corner, just as she said. The windows are plastered over with brown paper that's curling at the edges, and the sign above the window has a couple of letters missing — so it reads *P-o-n — -ntiques*.

She's right — I think it's supposed to say Phoenix Antiques, but it could just as easily say Polony Antiques if you squint. I suspect that naming an antiques shop after a cold slicing sausage isn't great marketing, so it's probably Phoenix. Anyway, there's a sign in the window saying the premises are available to lease, just as she told me, and I waste no time in making note of the details.

I've moved back to Edinburgh after a few years spent in Glasgow, and I am, genuinely, looking to expand my interior design business. As I told the girl in the bar, I don't like working for anyone else, I don't like taking orders and I've spent years building my own business up. I think I've taken it as far as I can in the west, and a foothold in the capital sounds ideal. It's time to come back properly, to swoop in and stake my claim in Edinburgh. And I'll fight for that with everything I have in my power.

And I've got a lot of power. It's an interesting twist of both fate and genetics, that of all the McCreadies, I'm the first-born; and alongside that comes a huge weight of responsibility. I'll confess here that I've had to learn how to use my questionable 'talents' — well — *responsibly*. Because there is, and I will admit this too, the chance that my darker side might just win if it tries hard enough to escape. And I know in many cases I can be a force to be reckoned with. That's just the way it is. But I usually achieve what I want to achieve without causing too much carnage. My three brothers and my little sister have all got their foibles — we're unique and we understand each other but it was, as you might imagine, quite a madhouse growing up.

And today, I decide that Polony Antiques is something worth swooping in on. That red-head is a dreamer. A beautiful, drunk, funny dreamer and she reminds me of things long ago — but my dark side sniggers a little and suggests that she'll never know, and what's the harm in a little swooping anyway? If it's Fate — well. You know how that goes. We *all* know how that goes.

As I jot the number down, I recognise the name alongside it and smile. I've got a good chance with this one. I rev my motorbike and speed off, grinning through the visor. Oh yes. This shouldn't be a problem at all.

# 2

## Liza

'Thanks very much,' I say, smiling into the receiver. 'I look forward to seeing you.'

'It might be me,' says the girl on the phone. 'Or it might be my boss, Mr Hogarth. It's more than likely to be me though. Mr Hogarth gets very busy and he often entrusts me with these tasks.'

'Great!' I say, warming to the girl's friendly voice. 'And you are?'

'Nessa. You'll know me when you see me.'

'Fantastic. See you tomorrow then!' I hang up on the girl and close down the browser on my laptop.

After that discussion with the guy in the bar, I went home and thought about it. And I decided, why not? The shop is perfect, and who knows whether I'll ever get a chance like this again? That little place has got the potential to be exactly what I imagine.

I can't wait to see what's behind those curling brown papers up at the windows. It's my absolute dream to have my own premises and sell books, paintings and antiques. I can see it now, emblazoned on the window — on that three-pane bay window: *books, paintings, antiques*.

## Scott

Yes, I can just see it now, emblazoned on the three-pane bay window: *fabrics, furnishings, décor*. It's going to be the ideal premises for my interior design outlet. And I think it's time I popped in to see my little sister Nessa — high time.

I park the motorbike just outside her house and head up the steps. It's a fabulous building, no denying that. A Georgian townhouse that was originally split into three flats — but Nessa and Ewan have renovated their way through the place and brought it back to how it was. I loved helping out with the decoration, although Nessa had told me I couldn't go into Ewan's man-cave on the attic floor, or her 'witchy consultancy' in the basement.

'It's my witchy consultancy,' she'd told me, glaring at me with her arms folded. 'It's not to be meddled with.'

'I don't even know what you need to witchily consult,' I'd said, exasperated by her, a ton of notebooks, sketch-pads and fabric samples in my arms.

'*I* don't consult, stupid boy,' she said. 'People come to consult *me*.'

I was slightly baffled but decided not to pursue it any further. Nessa's always been a bit eccentric but anything to do with witches is her area of interest, not mine. She was named after our great-great-grandmother who some said was a witch, and our Nessa has a bit of an interest in it all. We just let her get on with it. As I said, we've all got our foibles. I don't know how her Ewan puts up with it — he's an author and a DJ and melded the two together in yet another big-budget film that Guy Ritchie directed last year. I expect Ewan just hides in his man-cave, spins a few discs and writes his next bestseller.

'Make it nice, though,' Nessa had called after me that day, as I headed up the stairs into the living area. 'We're entertaining Vinnie and Jude and I want to make sure it's suitable.' I had hesitated for only a second. Knowing Nessa, she could easily have been referring to Vinnie Jones or Jude Law, but again, I didn't pursue it. Basically, because I knew she wanted me to.

But today, as I ring the doorbell, I'm whistling confidently and have my crash helmet under my arm, ready to greet her with the McCreadie Winning Smile. We five McCreadie spawn seem to possess this particular smile and use it to our great advantage. Or is that just me? Anyway, after a moment, the door

19

opens and something hairy is staring me in the face.

'Schubert was just going out for his constitutional,' my sister says, as it becomes clear that the hairy thing is her massively fat cat.

'Mow wow,' Schubert greets me, and leaps from her arms with surprising grace. He winds himself around my legs once or twice — with Schubert, I'm not sure whether it's a friendly greeting or an experiment to see if he can trip me up. Today, however, I step over him and he thumps off to wherever he goes for his constitutional. With Schubert, I've learned that you don't ask questions.

'What do you want, Scott?' asks Nessa, quite bluntly. She steps aside and I walk into the house and smile again.

She casts her gaze up and down me. 'You need a hair-cut,' she says.

I shake my head. 'No I don't.'

'I don't know how you get all that hair under your helmet. Like I told Aidan last month, long hair looks good on him. On you, it looks messy.'

I ignore her. I don't even ask if she means Aidan Turner, because I can see that's where it's going. My hair is jaw-length and dark and wavy, whereas hers is frizzy.

'You're just jealous, Ness. Because my hair isn't frizzy like yours.'

'Shut up, Scott,' she says and slams the door, but it's too late because I'm already in the house which was one of my objectives. The next is to get what I want from her. I turn and pull one of her corkscrew curls, letting it bounce back and grin. 'Just joking,' I say. 'Now, I was wondering if you could help with something.'

Nessa holds her forefinger up. 'Hang on,' she says. She turns to the staircase and bellows up it. 'Ewan! Scotty's after something. I told you, didn't I?'

There's a thud as the door to Ewan's man-cave opens and then he comes downstairs and pauses halfway, grinning at me, 'Hey Scott. She saw the bike pull up.'

21

'Yeah, no witchy magic in that, is there?' I say. 'How are you?'

'Great, great,' he says and nods. 'Just trying to fill in a plot hole.' He frowns and points over his shoulder, back upstairs.

'Hey, don't let me stop you!' I tell him. 'She's right — I do want something. I'll be here a while, so I'll catch you later, yeah?'

Ewan nods. 'Later. I'll head down when it's sorted.' He gives me a thumbs up and goes back upstairs, taking them two at a time. I'm not particularly short, at six-foot tall, but Ewan's got to have three or four inches on top of that, and I'm surprised he doesn't bump his head on the ceiling as he bounds upstairs.

'I suppose you want a cup of tea,' Nessa says grudgingly and waves me into the kitchen.

'If it's not too much bother.' I put my helmet down and sit at the table. The kitchen is 'Shaker' style and she's got a central island painted blue with a wooden top. It's all matched with the exposed fireplace and polished wooden floors, and there are big ceiling-to-floor French windows that open out onto the garden. I look around approvingly — I knew it would all work together.

Nessa flicks on the kettle and leans on the unit, her hands on her hips. 'So what *do* you want?'

'I want Polony Antiques.'

'Polony Antiques?' She gives me an odd sort of look. 'Where on God's green earth is that?'

'That corner shop on Methven Street — sorry, I think it's meant to be Phoenix Antiques, but the sign is dodgy.'

'Oh!' A light goes on in her face, but I haven't known Nessa all her life to think it's a pro-Scotty light. 'That might be spoken for, I'm afraid.'

'Spoken for?' I almost shout the words. 'But Nessa!'

'But Scotty. Just because Mr Hogarth is my boss, it doesn't mean that you can have all the property he owns.'

Nessa works for some mysterious guy called Mr Hogarth. I've never seen the chap, and I don't know what his first name is. I just know that when I pop in to see her if I'm in the area, he's never in the building — or at least there's a sign on her desk that says 'Mr Hogarth is out. Sorry'. She says it stops people asking silly questions. Mr Hogarth is a private detective by trade, but he seems to be a man of property as well. He's Nessa's landlord and Ewan's godfather and goodness knows how many other fingers he's got in pies, in and around Edinburgh.

'I don't want *all* the property he owns, Nessa,' I say, leaning forward and smiling again. Nessa twists her face and glares at me. 'I just want Phoenix Antiques. Don't you think it would be perfect for me to grow my business in?'

'Do you know, when you smile like that, you look like a sinister vampire?' is Nessa's only comment.

'Agnes Morag Flora McCreadie!' I explode. Nessa's face hardens. Maybe I shouldn't have used her full name.

'You simply *cannot* have the property, Scott. For one thing, it's not mine to give away. And for another, I'm not an estate agent. I work for a private detective. And for a third thing, I've got a lady interested in it who probably won't want it at a knockdown rental price.'

She turns away and I swear under my breath. I drum my fingers on the wooden work surface. I sometimes forget she's in her twenties now, and no longer the little girl I could coax into ribbons and pretty outfits. Yes, I briefly dallied with fashion design, but I'm happy that I settled on interior design — my dreams of flirting with a variety of models through Paris Fashion Week backfired and I found that they were more interested in the clothes than they were in me — at least houses don't act like divas. Some householders appreciate my Winning Smile and the way I have of talking to them as if they're the most beautiful, exciting client I've ever had.

It's maybe not an entirely ethical approach, like I say my dark side has much to answer for, but it's stood me in good stead.

However, my sister isn't taken in by my charms. Nessa slops a cup of tea in front of me and pushes a plate of chocolate digestives towards me. I push them away as I see a Schubert hair on the plate. I'm fairly sure one of them has been licked.

'But it's perfect.' I give Nessa a puppy dog stare, despite the fact that I know only one of my eyes is visible beneath my heavy fringe, and she shakes her head.

'No. I have to be fair. If the lady tomorrow doesn't like it, then I'll consider it. You're just a client, Scotty. Sorry.'

'I'm your big brother!' I protest.

'Exactly.' She folds her arms again. 'And you're the one who pulled the head off my teddy bear when I was three.'

I lower my eyes. I know for now the battle is lost.

# 3

## Liza

'Hello. I'm Miss Graham.' I hold my hand out to the girl who is standing by the entrance to the shop. Her dark, curly hair is blowing about in the breeze and her bright green eyes are friendly.

'Hello,' the green-eyed, dark-haired girl replies and shakes my hand firmly. She consults her clipboard. 'Miss Liza-Belle Graham?'

'Just Liza,' I say, 'to rhyme with Tizer.'

'Not Lisa like in Tower of Pisa,' says the girl. She nods and makes a mark on the clipboard. 'Good. Thank you. I'm Nessa McCreadie, we spoke on the phone. As you might know, Mr Hogarth is a very busy man and he is currently privately detecting. That's why he sent me along. I've got the keys and we'll have a look inside, shall we?'

I nod and feel a bubble of excitement in my stomach. I turn away from Nessa and have a look at the environment as she works on the locks, and I'm glad to see there's a little sort of shrubbery garden, separated from the shop by a cobbled path which, I think, leads into a little courtyard at the back; at least that's what it looks like on Google Maps. The shrubbery is waving a little, and I assume there must be a cat poking around inside it, as I glimpse something black moving around. I don't mind; I like cats.

'Mum, I'm away to have a look.'

Isa has demanded to come with me to check out the outside space, and it's all looking safely fenced off, so I'm good with that. It gives me time to have a look at the premises in peace, anyway.

'Okay. Well don't go too far. We'll just be inside.'

Even she can't fail to be impressed with the outside space. In my head, the path, the shrubbery and the courtyard are decorated with fairy lights, but not just for Christmas. In addition to that, I've got some tables and chairs out there for visitors to enjoy the summer sunshine. Because in my head, I've got a little tea-shop in the back room — if it's big enough inside, which I think it is. The prospect gives me more squiggles of excitement.

'That's it! Got it!' The door is old and creaky and Nessa has had to put her whole weight behind it to force it open, but she's managed, and we both step inside.

It's gloomy, otherworldly, freezing cold and smells of damp but I love, love, *love* it at first sight.

'There's a tea-shop!' I practically squeak and point to a little room down a couple of steps. 'I knew it!'

Nessa consults her clipboard again. 'It's not done out as a tea-shop,' she says. 'By that, I mean it's not got a kitchen or anything in it.' She frowns and flips some pages over. 'I think it used to be the staff office. But you could probably do it.' She looks up at me. 'I'm sure there's capacity.'

I just nod, staring around me. 'I love it.' I head towards the back of the shop and my nose starts to run as the cold air tickles it, but I don't care and practically skip down the steps. The back room, I see now, is actually two rooms — one small room tucked away next to the other, which means I have space for a kitchen and a tea-shop. 'And the top bit,' I say, indicating the big room Nessa is still standing in, 'can be the main shop. Perfect.' I visualise it with a set of antique bookshelves lining the wall, filled with lovely old volumes and modern-day stationery perhaps. Maybe some craft stuff, like packets of vintage scraps to stick in scrapbooks, or lino-printed postcards, or pretty handmade soaps. Then in my mind's eye, I see antiques scattered on other surfaces and clustered in the window. I can also imagine local artists having exhibitions on the walls, with photographs or textiles or traditional paintings, and my heart is hammering because the whole prospect is just mad and wild and I can so imagine myself doing it.

I might even start an art club — I could run it and teach it perhaps. Painting is my secret vice; something I've never managed to bring to the fore due to life getting in the way. Or I could get seriously into upcyling unwanted junk. I've always fancied a bit of that — a wee bit of decoupage or making shelves out of ladders. I especially fancy making lamps out of jam jars and string, and using tree branches to dangle them off. Or if people wanted to use the space for a book group, they could. That would be quite nice too.

'It's quite a touristy thoroughfare,' says Nessa, nodding as she looks around the building, 'so you'd get some footfall as well as local people coming. But I think you need more than just a shop to encourage people to come again, so a tea-shop would be lovely.

31

You could do a book group or something. An art club maybe. Rent out the space for functions.'

'I could indeed.' I smile. 'Definitely.' I turn around and head towards the back door, which is a dull sort of fire-door at the minute. In my imagination, my fairy lights lead out to a rose-draped wooden arbour, and a little flight of steps lead down to the courtyard. 'Can we just go out back and see what the space is like?' I know, I just know I have to go out there — it's like something buried deep inside me is straining to break free and burst out of that fire-door and my heart begins to pound . . .

'We can,' replies Nessa and fumbles on with her keys. 'It's this one, I think.' She fits it in the lock and eases the door open. 'After you,' she says and steps back.

Eagerly, I step outside.

And I scream as I come face to face with a hulking great, leather-clad brute wearing a motorcycle helmet.

# Scott

'Bloody hell!' I shout as this harridan bears down on me and screeches in my face. I'm glad I've got my visor down, as it's a layer of protection, of sorts.

My sister bursts out of the premises seconds after the harridan, and she screams too. Only she screams my name.

'Scott Alexander McCreadie! You idiot! I could have you arrested for trespassing!' she bellows.

'I'm not trespassing!' I yell back, but my voice is oddly muffled due to the visor, so I pull the helmet off and glower at my sister. 'I repeat. I am not trespassing.'

'Yes you are! Look — it was you who flattened the shrubbery, wasn't it? You who trampled soil around inside the garden and the courtyard. You who sneaked up the pathway and terrified my client.' Nessa points at the shrubbery. 'I've been private detecting myself for quite some time, Scott, and I know a thing or two. Mr Hogarth has talked to me about his cases and taken me on field trips. I can tell when something has been damaged by a six-foot-tall idiot in motorbike leathers!'

'I was just . . . looking around!' I begin to protest.

'Hang on!' The girl who screamed at me suddenly speaks and points her finger at me 'You! It's *you*. From the bar!'

I focus my attention on her, rather than my frizzy-haired sister and take a couple of seconds to realise it's the same girl who told me about the shop in the first place. This is a bit awkward. But maybe I'll be lucky and she won't realise that I think this premises is pretty much perfect for *my* little enterprise. I smile the McCreadie Smile, but I'm afraid that the power of the smile — and my own dark, devilish, usually irresistible power — doesn't seem to be working today, as her face doesn't relax at all. I hope I'm not losing my touch.

I think she's realised that *I* think it's pretty much perfect for my little enterprise.

Definitely awkward.

'Oh! Yes. So it is. It's *you* from the bar. Fancy that!' I say.

'I can't believe you came here,' she says in a low, dangerous voice. 'You *know* how excited I was.'

Well, I'm not standing for that.

I scowl at her and match my voice to hers. 'I *don't* know how excited you were, because all you did was *talk* about the place. You said, as I recall, 'I'll never do anything about it, but it's nice to dream.' You never said you were serious about it!'

She does me the honour of blushing and looking away. It's not a lie. She did say that.

'I went home and thought about it,' she snaps. 'It was too good a chance to miss. I didn't think you would stoop so low as to try and gazump me.'

This was hysterical if I'm honest, and I can't help it — I roar with laughter.

'Gazump you?' I cry. 'It's a rental property. There's no gazumping involved. Neither one of us is buying it, as far as I'm aware. And I'm fairly certain gazumping is kind of illegal in Scotland. I'm just having a look around to see if it would be suitable for my business — '

I don't get a chance to finish my sentence as she leans forwards and bellows at me. '*I'm* looking to see if it's suitable for *my* business! I saw it first!'

'So what?' I yell back. 'It's a free country.'

'Will you both just shut up!' screeches Nessa. She inserts herself between us, looking from one to the other. Then she turns to the girl and composes herself. 'I'm sorry. You're a client and I shouldn't shout at you like that. But you see, this is my older brother. I've known him all my life and it's terribly difficult to win an argument with him.' She turns and glares at me. 'I haven't forgotten the LuaLua incident and I never shall.'

'The LuaLua incident?' The girl from

the pub blinks, confused.

'It was a misunderstanding,' I say smoothly. 'Nothing to bother about.'

'A misunderstanding that made me look like an idiot,' replies Nessa. She points at me but addresses her client. 'He let me walk into a shop and ask if I could buy a LuaLua. I meant a Hawaiian lei, but he didn't tell me. He knew that I was asking the man if I could buy a professional footballer, and he didn't tell me. He's horrid.'

The girl looks shocked. 'I would *never* do that to *my* little sister,' she says, full of compassion. 'How awful.'

But there was something in her eyes that I recognise when I look in the mirror — that too-wide, too-innocent glance that you use to get people on your side.

'You haven't got a little sister, have you?' I ask her, accusingly.

'That's beside the point. If I did, I'd never do that to her.'

I shake my head and take hold of Nessa's arm.

37

I draw her to the side. 'Nessie, please. Let me at least have a look inside the place. I'm here now.'

Nessa sighs, quite theatrically. 'Mr Hogarth only expects me to entertain one client at a time.' She's putting obstacles in my way and we both know it.

I start to get a bit angry and scowl at her. I feel my inner demon beginning to wake up and grumble. 'I'm not a client, I'm your brother.'

She stands her ground. 'All the more reason not to be accused of nepotism.'

'You're living with Mr Hogarth's godson in one of his properties!' I explode. 'A *massive* property!'

Nessa folds her arms. 'It took a lot to get to that point, and nepotism was not part of the getting there.'

I look helplessly at the girl in the courtyard. She's chewing the comer of her nail and looking at us sceptically. I'm not going to cause a scene in front of her. She looks as if she'd live on that sort of story for years, trotting it out in

38

wine bars with her friends.

'Fine. You win.' I glare at Nessa and pull the helmet back on. It's flattened my fringe and I imagine I must look like a kind of motorbike pirate at the minute, with my hair covering one of my eyes like a patch, but I'm not going to give either of them the satisfaction of watching me pull the helmet off, adjust my hair carefully and pull it back on. I'd rather squint than make myself look stupid in their presence.

I turn angrily, the buckles on my boots jangling as I stomp my way across the tiny courtyard and down the little cobbled lane by the side of the building.

Nepotism! As if.

Good grief. I thought I could have expected better treatment from my own sister.

## Liza

I watch the demon biker disappear and I half expect the scene to end like a

Meatloaf video, in a puff of dry ice with a vampire maiden swooping down to reclaim her lover before night falls.

'Sluagh sidhe,' I mutter. I was brought up on tales of Celtic folklore — not surprising, considering my family lived in a tiny village where people (and indeed both my grannies, one of whom was Irish and one of whom was Scottish) still kept their west-facing windows shut in case these *sluagh* flew in. I had always thought they were fascinating creatures — evil fairy hosts who fought battles in the air and swarmed in at night to kidnap mortals, steal souls and take innocents down with them . . .

Nessa whips her head around and I feel my cheeks burn. I've just verbalised the thought that her brother is a thing of folklore — potentially a host of the undead, and most certainly a trouble-some and destructive creature.

'Our great-great grandmother was a witch,' Nessa says, throwing me. 'It's not impossible — but please remember that there is also a possibility that those people are fallen angels.'

'Fallen angels?' I stare at her. 'Less likely, I think. They're the souls of the undead! Can't be disputed.'

Nessa shrugs, unconcerned. 'It's a possibility. My family has been many things over the years. And with Scott being the eldest — well — perhaps all the angel charm was channelled into him first.'

This conversation is taking a very strange turn, so I think it's best if I change the subject before she starts questioning my upbringing and draws her own conclusions over that too.

'When will the property be available?' I ask. 'I think it may be just about perfect for my purposes, but I'll have to consider it.'

'Well it's available now,' says Nessa, flipping her paperwork around. 'But I would strongly suggest you don't dilly-dally.' She looks up at me and smiles. 'There's already been some more interest in it.'

41

'More interest apart from him?' I ask, nodding towards the pathway he disappeared down.

'I suspect so,' says Nessa with a smile. 'It's sometimes quite difficult to work with Mr Hogarth in these issues. He's a very busy man, and all contracts are signed with no recourse. I couldn't tell you who else was interested, even if I knew who it was and how many there were. He does keep a lot of things confidential. I suppose that comes with him being a private detective. People in that field aren't generally known for their public side. Discretion is nine tenths of the law, and all that.'

'I thought it was possession?' I'm slightly baffled.

'It might well be in some circles, but Mr Hogarth prefers discretion. Now, would you like to stay out here a little longer, or do you want to go back inside? I think there's a dear little studio flat upstairs as well — that's not in the bundle, as it were, but it can be negotiated separately. We can pop up and see it, if you want?'

'I want to,' I say quickly. 'I want to very much.'

# 4

## Scott

I'm not moving from this spot. Mr Hogarth isn't the only one who can stake out a place. I've got a perfect little area here, just hidden in the shadows, and I can study what's going on. I perch on my motorbike and fold my arms.

The windows upstairs aren't covered, and I see two figures appear in the big one above the entrance door. One dark frizzy head and one red curly head stand, backs to the outside world, having some sort of animated conversation, judging by the nodding heads and the hands flailing around as one or the other points to something. As far as I can remember though, the rooms upstairs weren't even in the deal. Great. Just great. The red-head even gets special privileges at looking into restricted areas.

I'd love to have a look in that place properly, but it's not even like I can contact Mr Hogarth himself because everything gets filtered through my sister.

After what seems to me like far too long, Nessa and the girl from the bar come back outside. The red-head is smiling and looking excited and I squash down happier thoughts of red-heads I used to know, and I can feel myself scowling. Nessa is chattering away to her and ushering her back along the street — but I notice that Nessa hasn't locked the door. On the contrary, she's only closed it to. It wouldn't take much for me to wait a moment until I'm sure the red-head has gone and sneak into the building. I can spend a bit of time in there myself and imagine how my samples and my design ideas would look.

Nessa places her hand in the small of the red-head's back, gently steering her away from the front door. I don't think I'm entirely imagining the fact that Nessa has looked straight at me, hidden away as I am in the shrubbery.

It's like there's a challenge in her eyes — or, more likely, a 'hurry up and do it. I have to lock up later, you know' look.

I smile at her, even though I'm fairly sure she can't see me — but it's a bit weird because she seems to smile back, then turns her attention back to escorting the client away.

'What are you doing in here?' I jump and swear as a thin, reedy voice challenges me.

'What the — ' I begin, then check myself as a child stands staring at me. She must be about ten years old and her hair is the same colour as my rival's in the antiques shop.

'I could tell on you,' the brat continues, staring at me defiantly. 'I could definitely tell on you.'

I glare at her. 'No you couldn't. You wouldn't know who to tell.'

'I'd tell my mum.' She points to the

shop the red-head has just left.

For a split second I'm astonished. The red-head has a child? 'Really?' I say. 'Well I'd tell on you. See that other lady? The one with the frizzy hair? Well that's my sister and she's in charge so . . .' I shrug nonchalantly and re-fold my arms.

'Hmm.' The child stares at Nessa for a minute. 'Well. I'm going. You should too.' She tosses her head back and her little curls bounce around like Miss Piggy's from *The Muppets*.

'I'll take my time, thanks,' I tell her and turn away from her. I can sense her pausing.

Is it wrong that I feel energised by winning a verbal battle with a brat? Maybe, but I do anyway. Or maybe the energy is coming from a different source, but I try not to think that way.

I wait until the brat saunters around the corner, and then I slip out of the bushes and run to the door. I touch it gently and it opens easily. I smile again;

I have my sister to thank for that, I think.

I step inside and the first thing that I notice is the silence — not just a normal silence, but the sort of silence that makes me think something might be lurking in the shadows watching me. It's not enough to unsettle me. That sort of thing rarely does, and I look slowly around the place, defying anything to come out and challenge me. Then I walk forwards into the room.

There's a sort of back room to the premises, and I make my way down the couple of steps into it. There's a faint trace of perfume: Nessa's, obviously, mingled with the rose-and-patchouli smell of the red-head's. There's a set of footprints in the dust, and I can see where they have wandered around, back and forth, then out into the courtyard where they spotted me.

I see the fire-door and put out a hand, pushing it gently, and that opens too, onto that courtyard. I don't go outside — I've explored the courtyard quite enough, and I know it'll look perfect for some statuary and outdoor sculptures, because it'll be quite easy for me to branch out into garden design, as well, I think. Or at least, design how pretty a garden will look after someone like a landscape gardener has sorted all the plant stuff out.

I close the door and turn back into the main part of the shop. I see a staircase tucked away in the corner, only visible from this room, and my heart pounds a little faster. This leads up to the first floor, and it's clearly where Nessa and the red-head went as there are more scuff marks in the dust.

Well, what's good for the goose is good for the gander, and I hurry up them myself, pushing open the door and entering a little maze of rooms. I think it's supposed to be a flat or something, but it's not very big. There's a sink and some old units in the corner of one room with a big window over the courtyard, so I guess this was kitchen/diner/lounge, then a sort of dog-leg

49

corridor leads into a smaller room which I suspect was a bedroom, and a corridor wiggles off that one into a bathroom — which, bizarrely, has another door connecting to the kitchen room. That makes sense, as you wouldn't want people trekking through your bedroom into the bathroom. I find myself back in the bigger room and turn a full circle. I can actually see, in my mind's eye, what a stunning little place this would be, even if it has got a yellowish, grimy skylight in the roof that's seen better days.

Maybe, once the business is up and running downstairs, I can convert this place and rent it out — either for holidaymakers or for someone who wants to live here on a more permanent basis. I wonder about the possibility of building a central point and putting a new skylight in — something that will spill even more light into the central hallway of my imagination, and be a bit of a feature. Triangles. I could go with a triangular sort of theme — like the glass pyramid above the Louvre. Oh yes.

The world is my lobster. I've just got to —

' — Mow *wow*!'

I yell as something big and fat and hairy thunders past me. If bloody Schubert was a thinner cat, I'd say he slunk past me, but I can't say that as he's huge.

'For God's sake, Schubert! Bloody cat!' I yell and Schubert fixes me with one of his obnoxious glares. I see there's a nick in the side of his ear which wasn't there before, and it looks like he's caught it on something.

'What the hell are you doing here?' I ask him, which is remarkably stupid as he's not going to answer me, but it does explain the creepy feeling of being watched downstairs.

I lean down and groan as I pick him up. He hangs there, his legs fixed vertically and his tail sticking out horizontally. I have never known a Beast like this thing, ever.

I peer at his ear and see it's not as

bad as it looks, although it's oozing a bit of blood. Nessa is going to freak out when she sees this. Speaking of which, the magic has disappeared and now reality is me lugging this Thing downstairs and trying somehow to return it to its owner. He must have followed her here —

' — he must have followed me here.' Nessa is at the bottom of the little staircase, looking up at me. 'Schubert. Scotty doesn't want to play. Put him down.'

I stumble a little, wondering if I heard that correctly, but before I can process it, Schubert compounds matters by letting out a pathetic catty wail. 'Mow *woooowwww*,' he moans and suddenly goes all floppy and weak in my arms.

'Oh, my baby! What have you done to your ear?' Nessa swoops in and relieves me of Cat-Burden and I flex my fingers, wondering how my little sister can lug that Thing around as much as she does.

'I have no idea what he's done,' I tell Nessa. 'He was upstairs and I think he's caught it on something, but I don't think it's too bad.'

Nessa is cooing over and petting the Beast, and he's lapping it up. 'He must have been trapped upstairs, poor little mite,' she says, hugging him to her and nuzzling into his face as he nuzzles pitifully back. I grimace, thinking of the warm tuna-breath Schubert is breathing onto her. 'I thought he had come here, I just knew he would. He was very interested when I discussed it with him,' she continues. 'That's why I left the doors slightly open, so he could come home when he'd finished exploring. Dear Schubert.'

She doesn't look at me, and I wonder if she's just saying that so I don't think she's engaged in any sort of nepotism whatsoever.

'I wouldn't have left the doors open so *you* could poke around,' she says, 'because that would be engaging in nepotism and I don't do that.' She nuzzles Schubert again, and shifts his weight a bit. He somehow scrambles up her body and crawls around her neck so he lies there, looking like a fox-fur, as she finds the keys for the building. 'We have to leave,' she says, and I'm not sure whether she's addressing me or the cat. 'Come along, darling.'

It's the cat, then.

Nessa glares at me. 'And *you* can leave too. Or I *will* have you done for trespassing.'

I am, literally, speechless.

But it's best not to argue.

## Liza

'Mum, there was a weird man.'

Isa thinks this a perfectly acceptable opening to a conversation over dinner, and I freeze. What if there was some weird man stalking the children around school? Or when they're out playing in the park? Or on the bus when they come home from school, riding in a

54

ceaseless loop, all the better to see all the kids, all day, every day, on the bus route.

'A weird man?' I repeat. 'Where?'

'At the place we were at today,' says Isa. She spoons some spaghetti bolognese into her mouth and chews thoughtfully. 'I told him I'd tell on him.'

The penny drops. 'Ah. The weird man. Did he have dark hair and was he wearing black clothes?'

'That's him.' Isa nods and tucks into some garlic bread. 'He said he would tell on me as well, so we just called it quits in the end.'

I choke slightly and wash my own pasta down with a glug of water. 'I see. He's not really weird,' I say carefully. 'I kind of know him. I've met him before. He was interested in the shop, I think.'

Isa nods again. 'I hope you get the shop and not him.'

'Me too,' I say. 'It's a nice shop, isn't it?'

'I quite liked the garden. I could have a swing out there.' Her eyes drift over to the unkempt little yard at the back of our flat. I keep meaning to do something with it, but it's difficult to get the time when you're working and looking after a child.

It wouldn't be so bad if Isa's father was around, and I could send her there for a weekend every so often, but Isa was the product of a drunken night out when I was a student at the University of West Scotland.

My grannies hissed and cursed and did a sign to ward away evil when I told everyone where I was going. They hated the west and the idea of the *sluagh sidhe* with a passion — but me, well, I couldn't wait to get the hell out of our tiny village in Inverness-shire and get as far west as I could. I don't know what the pull was over that way, but I just knew I had to go. It was like a gossamer thread was dragging me towards it. Like I knew something was waiting for me, and I needed to grab it, if only Fate would concur.

Instead, I ended up sleeping with

Isa's father. So maybe she was the reason I had to go there — so I could bring this incredible force of nature into the world? Who knows. It was certainly very different to any other one-night stand I'd had, and I must confess I'd had a few before then. But that one, the one with Him, was the last one.

I've given the man a lot of thought over the last decade or so; and even more so recently, as I see less and less of me in my daughter and more of someone else. Or perhaps she's just becoming her own person. I'm not sure, but sometimes I look at her and wonder who she is. It might sound strange but sometimes I feel like she's an old soul who's been on this earth before.

And anyway, next door's yard is despicable — full of rusted metal and crap and I don't even know if I'd be happy letting Isa play out there properly.

But even though I'm trying to think of practical things, like junk-strewn yards, my mind refuses to co-operate and instead rolls back eleven years or so to the night Isa was conceived.

I think the guy, her father, was on a music course, but I couldn't swear to it. I remember there was a guitar in the corner of the room, because I fell over it on the way out and bent one of those things they use to tune it up. It seemed like the funniest thing in the world at the time — until the next day when I realised I had a huge gash down my leg where I'd subsequently ricocheted into the corner of a glass coffee table. I've still got a bit of a scar there. In the end, I handed my dissertation in when I was eight and a half months pregnant, and Isa came the next week, so I was bloody lucky, really.

Isa's got a natural talent for music that certainly doesn't come from me, so that's my thoughts on her biological father, anyway. I do recall he had a huge tattoo on his back though — it was some sort of skull with wings coming out of the sides and roses all around it. I caught a glimpse of it when . . . well, never mind. That's all ancient history. I got Isa and, looking at it very objectively, he got off scot-free. I spent months in a shared student house, getting fatter and fatter, reduced to wearing nothing but stretchy leggings and tops that strained across my ever-increasing girth as I tried to complete assignments, wedged uncomfortably behind my computer. I waddled heavily into lectures, burning with embarrassment as everybody averted their gaze — I could almost hear their thoughts as I struggled to fit into those silly deskseat combos, and they wondered how Liza-Belle Graham, party girl extraordinaire, had been brought so low.

As my friends moved on and moved away and coupled up and had children, I suddenly realised I'd never even had the pleasure of telling my partner we were having a baby. I wondered how that would feel. I wondered if it would be terrifying, but terrifying in an incredible, excited kind of way, as opposed to as terrifying as realising you're going to have to do it all on your own.

'Mum, what will you sell in the shop? If you get it?' asks Isa, interrupting my reverie.

'Books, paintings and antiques. Just like I always wanted to do.' I smile at my redheaded daughter. She's got emerald-green eyes, quite unlike my brown ones. She must have got those from her father as well. 'You should never give up on your dreams, you know. It's taken me ten years, but I *am* going to do it.'

My job at the minute pays the bills, but I don't want to work at a vet's forever. Don't get me wrong, being a vet's receptionist isn't too bad, most of the time, and it's within walking distance of my flat. But I don't like little rodent-y things like hamsters and gerbils and mice and rats. Dogs are fine. Cats are fine. Even birds to some extent, although I get conscious of their beady eyes settling on me in the waiting room. But little things with tails or tiny claws, small animals that poop out raisins and mess all over their cages and eat their young ... No. Just no. Isa wants a rabbit, and I won't even go down that route. Baby rabbits are ugly, hairless little creatures and I can't get over that image at all. One of our clients brought their rabbit in, and it gave birth right in the surgery. Ugh.

But on the other hand, I think how lovely it is that I'm able to sit here, after the mistakes I made in my early twenties, and tell the result of the worst of those nights that she can follow her dreams. Sometimes, I think I've cracked the parenting lark.

But Isa spoils the moment by rolling her eyes. 'You're always saying things like that to me!' she moans. 'I've told you. I'm going to be in a rock band and that's the way it is. I'm *never* going to give up my dreams.'

Did I forget to mention that she's headstrong as well? I'd say she didn't get that from me, but, well, let's not go there.

# 5

## Scott

I'm over at Nessa's again, standing in the lounge, engaged in a staring contest with Schubert. He's lying on the sofa and I want to sit there, but I'm damned if I'm asking a cat to move. Because Schubert is the sort of animal that you would have to ask, not one that you could just move or simply lift up out of the way.

'Dear Schubert. Will you let my Scott sit down?' Nessa drifts in with a briefcase and a superior expression on her face.

'Mow wow,' agrees Schubert and slides onto the floor in one fluid movement, where he lies prostrate, gazing up adoringly at Nessa and purring like a chainsaw. She leans down and rubs his neck and his eyelids flicker in ecstasy.

'Thank you,' she tells him, and indicates that I may sit. 'I usually transact business in Mr Hogarth's agency, as you know,' she continues, 'but this time I am going to make an exception, because you're my brother. This time, I am happy to tell you that Mr Hogarth has agreed that you can have the premises. I just need you to sign here, please.' She brings out a piece of paper and hands me a pen. 'Just on the dotted line please.'

I cast a quick glance at the proffered paperwork: 'No.' I say. I put the pen down.

'No?' She looks at me in astonishment. '*No?*'

'No,' I repeat. I nod at the paper. 'Not until you unfold it and I can read it.'

'Unfold it?' She's playing dumb and she's anything but. 'This? Unfold *this*?'

I feel my nostrils flare and I have to fight to control my voice because I know I am going to lose my temper. 'Yes. Please.'

'Oh.' She looks at the paper, which is

indeed folded in the middle, displaying a very sharp crease. 'I don't know if I can do that,' she says. 'Protocol dictates — '

' — *Protocol?*' I hiss. I lean forward. 'What exactly are you trying to hide from me?'

Nessa has the grace to look embarrassed. 'Well I suppose you've been a successful business person in your own right for several years,' she admits. 'It's not easy to be deceitful with you.' She sighs and unfolds the paper. There is space on the top half for another signature. I see there is a name printed alongside the dotted line. *Liza-Belle Graham.*

'And this means?'

'This means . . . ' She looks at the paper and smooths it out again, and I know she's playing for time. 'This means that Mr Hogarth is happy for you to have the . . . the *top* floor of the premises, but the proviso is Miss Graham has to have the *bottom* floor. You get to share the courtyard, though. That's nice, isn't it?' She looks up at me and the full force of her McCreadie

Winning Smile is met by stony contempt on my part. The McCreadie Smile seems not to be as effective on other McCreadie family members at the minute. Funny, that.

'And what does Miss Graham say to that?' My voice is cold.

'She doesn't know yet.'

'Okay. Well I suggest you speak to Miss Graham and explain it to her, and if *she's* willing to sign it, that's when *I'm* willing to sign it.' I put the pen down and fold my arms, confident that nothing of the sort will happen.

'Well you can tell her yourself,' Nessa says haughtily. 'She's due here in about five minutes.'

Schubert looks shocked and superior as I swear loudly in the middle of my sister's lounge.

## Liza

'It's quite a posh house, isn't it?' Isa is standing on the top step, gazing up in awe at the lovely townhouse before us. Then she grabs hold of the railings and almost tips herself upside down trying to see into the basement windows.

'Wow, that looks *cool* down there,' she exclaims. 'There's jars of all sorts on the windowsill. Like dried flowers and herbs. I wonder if it's drugs?' She rotates even further over the railing and I get hold of her shoulders and pull her back again.

'I'm sure it's not drugs,' I tell her.

The door has opened silently as I'm yanking her back and a pleasant voice welcomes us. 'No, the drugs moved out when the downstairs neighbours moved out. They went to Glastonbury. The neighbours that is. Not the drugs. Well, the drugs probably went too. I don't have any down there. I consult. I don't do drugs.'

I stare at Nessa McCreadie who is smiling at us, a black cat draped around her shoulders. 'It's my witchy consultancy,' she explains further and stands back. 'A long-time dream of mine come true. Because they can do, you know. Dreams can come true, that is; it's just sometimes weird how you get there.'

'Is that your witch's cat?' asks Isa, excitedly.

'I imagine that's how he would describe himself,' replies Nessa. 'He's called Schubert. Come in, please do. As I explained in my email, I'm working from home today. And we have rental paperwork. Yay!' She beams at us and claps her hands.

'Mow *wow!*' adds Schubert the witch's cat, raising his head and looking right at us. He's not a cat I recognise from our vet's at any rate, but he seems forthright and pleasant enough. I've learned enough about cats to recognise a pleasant one when I see one, rather than one who will have your leg off with its claws if you walk too close to it.

'Okay,' I say and smile. 'I think I'm ready to sign it.' I step inside, ready to commit to my dreams like something is pulling my very soul into that house — and a great, hulking black thing looms up out of the shadows.

It's him again — the demon biker — and I stiffen.

'You might not want to sign it when you see what they've done to the contract,' the biker growls.

I swear inwardly, my stomach churns and my soul goes *twang*, right back inside my body. 'And you're here, because?' I ask, coldly.

'Because it needs both our signatures if either one of us wants it. Isn't that right, Nessa?' The man is glowering at Nessa who looks serene.

'Mr Hogarth has his reasons,' she replies and smiles again. 'Now come in while we discuss it, in this rather unorthodox manner, in light of Mr Hogarth's instructions.'

Part of me wants to turn around and stomp off down the steps and into the street and throw things. But part of me wants to brazen it out and see what the demon biker means. His green eyes are drilling into mine again, a glower of the highest order on his sharp features.

I look again and I realise he hasn't really got sharp features — it's just that his cheekbones are way better than mine, so he has the most incredible hollows and shadows on his face. His chin is pretty square, actually, and his mouth would probably have a soft look to it if he wasn't glaring at me. He has laugh lines at the corners of his eyes, which I find astonishing as I don't know whether he even seems capable of genuine laughter.

Regardless, I set my lips to match his and draw my brows together and glower back. 'I don't know if those are terms I can accept,' I snap.

'You don't know what the terms are,' says Nessa and steps backwards, inviting me in. Schubert slithers off her neck like satin and rubs up against Isa's ankles. He looks up at her and purrs. Then he sort of marshals her inside the house — I'm not sure how he does it, but I'm reminded slightly of highly intelligent sheepdogs herding flighty lambs.

'Come on, Mum,' she says, and disappears into the hallway, full of confidence. She stops just inside and bends down. She picks the animal up and cuddles it. I'm astonished that she can even hold it, but maybe it's one of those cats who looks fat but is largely made up out of fur.

'Mow wow,' says the cat and rubs its face against Isa's.

'He knows a kindred spirit when he sees one,' says Nessa indulgently, and turns a bright smile onto me. 'Come on. This way, please.'

I seem to have no choice but to follow her.

The demon biker melts back out of the shadows and looms back up on my right-hand side. I shudder involuntarily. I tell myself it's repulsion, but a tiny, well-hidden kernel suggests it might be something else. Just to be sure, I stride away from him so I'm not too close.

'In here,' says Nessa. She pushes open a door and we're in a lounge. 'I don't want to keep you here too long, so I'm not going to invite you and Scott into the office. Having said that, Ewan was on a conference call to dear Martin earlier, and the line crackles a bit from the West Coast. Leo could hardly hear him, so Ewan is trying to sort that out, and I don't like to disturb him in the office.'

'My aunt lives in Cornwall,' I say. 'Sometimes you ring her, and she says there's a seagull on the wire and it makes the line bad.'

'California,' mutters Mr Cheekbones. 'It's *that* west coast. And it'll be Scorsese and di Caprio, so don't even engage her.'

I think there's an audible *clunk* as my jaw drops, and I catch what looks almost like a smirk on his face. Nessa doesn't seem to notice.

Instead, she puts a piece of paper on a coffee table and hands me a pen. 'Dotted line, up there, please, Liza. Scotty, you sign at the bottom as we discussed. The terms are as follows. Mr Hogarth is reluctant to lease the premises to either one of you on an individual basis, so Liza gets the shop floor, the tea-shop bit, etc, etc, and Scotty gets the upper floor. You share a staircase — of course — and you share the courtyard. Deal?'

She smiles brightly, and I put the pen down. 'No.' I fold my arms. 'Absolutely not.' I glare at — him — Scotty — and shake my head. 'Do you think I could go in to work every day and see him — *that* — smarming around upstairs? Knowing that he snuck in under false pretences and tried to steal my shop from under my nose?'

'Likewise,' he chips in. He folds his arms as well. 'Just what I said. I'm not sharing the place with *you*.'

'My, my.' Nessa shakes her head and folds her arms. We must all look like idiots. I unfold my arms and shove my hands in my pockets. He does the same, but Nessa remains with hers folded. 'You're both acting rather ungratefully. This is the best Mr Hogarth can do under the circumstances. He wants to please everyone. He's a lovely man. And you won't even give him the opportunity to help you both?'

The question is clearly rhetorical, but I feel my cheeks burn like I'm getting told off for missing my curfew or something. I look at the floor, thinking I should maybe say something in my defence because, after all, isn't Nessa kind of *working* for me? I snap my head up again meaning to come out with a scathing remark, but before I can, a reproachful 'Mow wow,' comes from Schubert and I look at him instead. I swear he is shaking his head.

Isa snorts a laugh and cuddles him even more. 'Isn't he cool? I think you should do it, anyway. I'm never going to get a swing otherwise.'

'A swing? A *swing*?' It's Scott's turn to speak and he stares at Isa. 'Do kids still play on swings?'

'They do if they're given the opportunity,' my daughter says, quite haughtily, and it's my turn to stare at her.

'Isa! That's a very rude thing to say,' I scold.

'Well it's true,' she says. 'I'd *love* a swing.'

'Mow *wow*,' agrees Schubert, vehemently.

But Scott is still staring at Isa cuddling the cat and being stand-offish and attitudinal — if that's even a word — and his eyes have gone wide for a second. Then he blinks and shakes his head. He stares at Nessa for a moment and she stares back. I feel like someone is going to draw a gun — it's the OK Corral in The Grange.

'If I do this,' he growls, turning his attention on Isa, 'and you *get* a swing there, you'll have to go on it enough to make it worthwhile and let us get on with business. No daft call outs for pushes on it. Nessa was awful for that.'

'I liked to go *high*,' says Nessa, equally haughtily, and Scott just narrows his eyes dangerously and shakes his head.

He glares at me and I glare back and

even so I know what's coming. I really want that place, and to be fair I hadn't even realised it had an upstairs until quite recently. Maybe I can get the stairs boxed off eventually, so he can't bother me.

'I'll do it,' he says. 'As an experiment. But if it's ridiculous and I can't stand it, I'm not paying your bloody boss a penny.'

'Me too.' I surprise myself by saying. 'As an experiment only. If *he* does my head in — ' here I point to *him* dramatically, ' — I'm not paying a penny either.'

'So, does that mean I get a swing?' persists Isa, her emerald eyes boring into me, as if she's trying to hypnotise me. She fails.

'We'll see,' I say coldly. And I take the pen (and I swear the cat has lifted a paw and nudged it my way) and sign my name: *Liza-Belle Graham*.

I put the pen down. I'm not handing it to him.

He takes it and leans over, reading

the words on the page. He shakes his head and sighs before scrawling his signature: *Scott Alexander McCreadie*.

'There. Done. Or do you want it signed in blood?' he growls as his eyes flash at Nessa.

Nessa smiles sweetly and refolds the contract. She pops it in her briefcase and clicks the latches shut.

'Not today,' she replies sunnily. 'Not today.'

# 6

## Liza

I have the sparkly new key in my hand so I can unlock my new premises and I've dragged Isa here as well — she complained about child labour, but I ignored her.

I'm all fizzy with lemonade bubbles of excitement as we approach the shop — and then I see a big white van emblazoned with *Scott McCreadie Interior Design* around the corner, and the lemonade bubbles just turn into nasty, gas-filled pockets of heartburn and I wonder for the umpteenth time why the hell I agreed to such an idiotic scheme.

'Ah. Good morning.' The way Scott McCreadie greets me is as if there is nothing good about it at all. He emerges from the back of the van, and scowls at me as he shoves a toolbox into the cavernous depths. He's got some rolled up papers which might, I suppose, be plans, and some sample books full of swathes of fabric. He's also got a pile of shiny, shiny interior design magazines which, in another world, I'd lust over, sighing happily as I flicked through the pages in my perfect, perfect home. But I'm not going to let him know that I'm even remotely interested.

'I'm going in the courtyard,' announces Isa. She's planted herself right between us. 'Because I can. Because it's shared.'

'Be careful,' I warn her. 'There's nothing there to interest you yet, so don't get into mischief. Or at least do some weeding to help out!'

But she's already vanished along the side of the building. I decide to ignore Scott McCreadie and his snazzy interior design swag and go straight through into the shop, although I feel a bit cheated that I can't use my key. It's very dusty inside, and you can tell that someone — him, probably — has been moving around in the building as there are lots of biker-boot type scuff marks on the floor, and motes dancing on the shafts of light coming in through the windows.

The back doors are closed, and here, at least, I can use my own key and throw them open. I walk through the building and down the little steps and fit the key in the lock. I shove the doors open and stand in the space, looking out onto the courtyard. My heart lifts as I see, in my mind's eye, the raised beds filled with flowers and herbs, the arbour with the fairy lights, the outside seating area, the swing . . .

Hang on.

The swing?

There's already a swing there.

And my daughter is pushing herself way up high on it, her red hair flying out behind her.

'Look, Mum! Look!' she shrieks as she swoops down and up, up and down.

I'm horrified. She's going to flip right over the top if she's not careful. 'Look!'

Then she launches herself off the thing as it arcs, landing neatly on her feet like Nessa's sodding cat.

With all the grace of a ballet dancer she drops down in a curtsey and picks up a wrench. 'What's this?' She looks up at me and trots over, her cheeks flushed and — almost — a smile on her face. 'D'you think someone left it here?'

'That'll be mine, thank you,' says Scott, as he looms up behind me and makes me jump.

He holds out his hand and Isa grins, handing the implement over. 'Did you forget it?' she asks. 'After you'd set the swing up?'

'I didn't set the swing up,' he replies, looking straight at her. 'The men did. I only came over and tightened up a couple of nuts.'

'Thanks,' she says. 'It's a really good swing.'

It *is* a really good swing, I have to agree. There's the swing, then there's like a wooden tower with a slide running down it in the middle, and a sort of see-saw on the other side of the tower. It won't have been cheap.

I gawp at it and turn to Scott, who is staring at the wrench in his hands very intently, looking like he might want to hit something with it. But I realise it's just a general, thoughtful glower.

'Thank you,' I say in a low voice, although I think I'm going to choke on the words. 'How much do I owe you?'

He shrugs his shoulders. 'Nothing.'

'Nothing? But you must have bought it and paid for it.' I'm now gawping at him.

'I did.'

'So . . . how much do I owe you?' I nod to Isa who has dashed back over and is scrambling up the climbing frame bit behind the tower. 'She's the one who'll be using it.' In my head, I'm frantically doing mental maths to see where the money will come from. It'll have to come from my capital — from the stock money.

'You don't owe me anything,' he says and looks directly at me and there's that weird little *twang* deep inside me again. I try hard to ignore it. 'It needed doing, and the courtyard is shared, as our landlord made clear. You can arrange the picnic tables for your tea-shop. I won't be having anything to do with those.'

He turns on his heel and stalks away. His buckles aren't jangling on his boots today; that must be because he drove a van instead of a bike, I think, almost randomly. I start to go after him, to pursue the conversation, but then I don't. I just stare after him as he disappears pointedly around the side of the building. He clearly doesn't want to go through my premises. I feel my cheeks burn and wonder if I'm being a Bad Person. It was a kind thing to do, really.

He didn't have to. But he did.

I wonder, fleetingly, if it's a metaphoric olive branch and frown at those thoughts. I tap the new paintbrush I've brought with me against my thigh and keep staring.

There's just something . . . something that's niggling at me about him, and I'm not quite sure what it is yet.

## Scott

Isa is still swinging. I can see her through the window upstairs as I sit at a makeshift desk and organise my computer. I've propped the door open as it needs airing in here, and I've forced the windows wide. The through breeze is quite pleasant.

God knows I need something to cool me down, because being so close to my fellow leasee has made me think of *her* again. Of the girl I let go, so long ago. It's the hair. It has to be. I didn't know that girl well enough to get to know her soul, but what I did see, I fell for — and fell for in a big way. Which was something I always guarded myself against.

I really can't let myself go where my mind wants to take me, so I scowl my very worst scowl and try to think of more practical things.

I need to do some work on the plans and see how I can fit a triangular structure up top. I wonder if there's some special glass coating I can get which shimmers and would reflect the colours in the sunshine, which in turn would make the triangle glow. I suddenly smile as I look at the screen and play around with options. This, *this* is my comfort zone. It's somewhere I'm confident in and somewhere to lose myself.

The only problem is the construction would take a few days to do, and Liza would probably complain, but I suppose could get it sorted for during the week when Isa's at school, and then at least the little one wouldn't be inconvenienced.

I pause and stare out of the window. She's really going for it with that swing. If she didn't have her mother's colouring, I could almost think it was Nessa, twenty years ago, doing the same thing. It makes me smile, and I shake my head before turning back to the computer.

'Sorry to disturb you.' There's a voice from the open doorway and I jump. I think the smile must still be on my face as Liza sort of bares her teeth in a way that makes me think it was an automatic response until she realised what she was doing.

I try to put the scowl back on my face, but suddenly it seems like too much effort.

Instead, I just lose the smile, make my face normal and lean back in the chair, my arms raised and my fingers locked behind my head. I look at her. 'That's fine,' I tell her. She waits in case I wish to elaborate on the comment, but then seems to realise I'm not going to.

She takes a step into the room, uninvited. 'I just want to say thank you for the swing set. I know it's not really for Isa, but it'll keep her out of mischief while I do some work on this place.'

I nod. 'That was the idea. Actually . . . while you're here, I just need to ask you something.' Her eyebrows shoot up into her fringe and a look of panic comes across her face. I fight back the temptation to laugh at her expression and instead continue with my conversation. 'I want to get some structural work done. I want to change that skylight.' I nod upwards and her eyes follow. I wait until she looks back at me. 'So, it'll be a bit disruptive. What days do you plan to work here over the next few weeks? I'll try to do it when you're not around.' I flick my gaze to the paintbrush she's still clutching. 'I know you're busy with stuff.'

'Well, it'll just be weekends at the minute. I'm negotiating with work to reduce my hours, but they need to contact the agencies first and get someone in to cover.'

'Okay. I'll sort it out ASAP then.' I unlock my fingers and pull myself upright again, shuffling my seat closer to the computer. 'Thanks,' I offer as an afterthought.

She nods. 'Just one thing. Planning permission. Or lack thereof.'

'Mr Hogarth. All sorted for anything we want. According to Nessa anyway. We're apparently good to go.'

She pauses and nods again. 'Okay. That makes sense.' A frown shadows her face, then she shakes her head and I hide a smile. It seems that she's learning about the elusive, yet omni-present, Mr Hogarth.

'Great.' I look at her and she stares back at me. She opens her mouth, then closes it again.

'I'll be downstairs,' she says and walks away. I hear her thumping down the stairs and I've got to admire her. She didn't have to come up here and face her mortal enemy.

I concentrate back on the computer. I'll have to get things moving quickly. I don't want my workmen coming in and messing up her paintwork, because that's just inviting trouble. Maybe she should start in the back room just in case.

I swear and push my chair back. I hurry to the top of the stairs and see her right at the bottom.

'Liza,' I shout. She turns and looks surprised. 'I'd start at the back of the shop if I was you. Stop the workmen making a mess of your paintwork.'

'Thanks. I'm already thinking of that,' she calls back. 'Maybe when you've finished with them, you can point them my way so I can get the kitchen and things sorted?'

'Maybe.'

We stare at each other for a moment, then she nods again and walks back into the shop.

I don't think I'll get those particular workmen to do the kitchen for her. She needs specialists.

I go back to the computer and start searching my contacts for kitchen appliance fitters and renovators.

If I pull some strings, it'll get all her

jobs sorted quickly, which means we can open for business sooner. I set my jaw again, battering down the thought I'm doing it to be kind and not just to get the job done.

# 7

## Liza

I'm fed up of the fact we have had workmen coming and going for what seems like fifty years, although I do appreciate the fact that Scott managed to get me a good deal on the fittings and things.

But in all that time — well, maybe it's only been a fortnight, but who's counting? — neither myself nor Isa have been allowed to sully his sacred space in the rooftop.

Mind you, I haven't allowed him to sully my sacred space either, which is now pretty much looking like a kitchen. It almost choked me to thank him out loud for sending the fitters my way, but I did, and he sort of nodded brusquely and said as payback we had to put up with the building work upstairs and not disturb him.

Which we have done, but even when I stand across the road and try to see what they're doing up there, I can't really tell. But the scaffolding and the flapping tarpaulins have been driven away on the back of a lorry half an hour or so ago, and I'm determined not to go outside and try to see it again. I don't want to give him that satisfaction.

So, to distract myself, I'm arranging some of my beautiful vintage china sets on the duck-egg blue shelves of my new tea-room, and I might even have a little play with my new coffee machine. It's in place ridiculously early, but hey — I need to be confident with it, don't I? Before we open. I feel a little squiggle of excitement as the milk nozzle thing goes *pssshshhhh* and, like magic, I have a lovely, foamy cappuccino in a cream-and red-spotted mug.

'Liza?' I hear him before I see him. I also hear his big, clumpy boots thumping down the stairs and cast a quick glance at my beautiful crockery displays, because it's typical that the vibration of his stompy feet will rattle them all and send them all bouncing to the floor.

'In here.' I quickly lick the spoon I've used to stir my coffee before he reaches me. However, he's quicker than I thought, and he's there, in front of me whilst I still have an apostle spoon hanging out of my mouth.

'Good look.' He nods. 'Not going to catch on though. Where's the brat?'

'Outside.' I gesture with the spoon. 'Not sullying your sacred space.'

'Sacred space be damned,' he mutters, and again I get that weird feeling that I've met him in folklore, and can kind of imagine him storming off on a wild hunt with the other *sluagh sidhe* as he charges past me, intent on locating my daughter.

'Brat!' he yells at the back door, and it's annoying, as he's right in the doorway and I couldn't get past him even if I wanted to. I take a sip of coffee and see if he can get her to come in, because I couldn't just before.

'What?' Isa's voice carries across the outdoor space and I cringe at how abrupt she sounds.

'I need you to have a look at something!'

There's a tiny, tiny beat. 'Okay.'

'Okay?' I splutter. 'She's coming in because you asked her to?'

'Seemingly.' He turns to me and flashes a quick smile that makes me blink and my coffee cup pause halfway to my mouth. There's just something there that I recognise, and it knocks on the door of my memory. As well as making me clutch my cup tighter as he looks — well — bloody attractive — with his black leathers on and his black T-shirt and his boots and that hair blowing suddenly in a wind that wasn't there before and his eyes flashing green at me . . .

I curse inwardly and shakily put my cup down on the bench. That smile is making me go places I don't want to go.

God forgive me, but I've even found myself waking up suddenly in the night and thinking of the *sluagh sidhe* carrying me back with them to the west. Does that mean I'm a lost soul? I've no idea anymore.

But Scott's voice brings me back to earth with a bump. 'I'm just taking her upstairs to see what she thinks of it.'

Isa is standing beside him. 'It'll be cool. Really cool if it's like what you said it was,' she says excitedly, and grins back up at him.

I have to turn away — she completely trusts this guy, doesn't she? Maybe I need to put aside my pre-conceived ideas and try to like him a little more myself. Not be scared of how he makes me feel and how he makes me remember how I felt that night, the night I let a green-eyed stranger make love to me; even though much of it is blurry around the edges.

*It won't be hard. It won't be hard at all*, a little voice inside tells me.

'Actually — ' He taps his fingers on

his chin thoughtfully. 'You can come too.' He points at me and narrows his eyes and I blink rather stupidly.

'Okay.'

'Okay. I think you might like it.'

'*Mrrffff . . .*' is all I can manage. Like an automaton I nod and find myself following them upstairs.

And when we get there, Isa shrieks in joy and starts pointing upwards. 'Mum! Mum! Look! Isn't that just the *best* thing ever?'

I follow her gaze . . . and we have a mini Louvre pyramid on the roof!

'Wow! Aye. Aye, it is. Wow.' I have to admit that I actually love it!

'Come on, Mum. Let's stand underneath it and look *up*. Look up at the sky. Can you imagine it at night — like when it's all dark and starry, and when the moon is out?'

And I can imagine it. I can imagine it very well, even though the sky is a bit grey and miserable today.

'Come on. The brat has a point.' Scott's voice is in my ear and it gives me a weird shiver, then I feel someone taking my hand. Then someone takes my other hand and all three of us are standing underneath the glass pyramid. All three of us are holding hands, which is kind of awkward, I guess, in some ways.

But Scott has, surprisingly, a firm, warm grip, and I just know that my hand will feel cold when he eventually lets go. I'm clutching Isa with my other hand. She tugs at us both and insists we walk around in a circle, really slowly.

So we do, in a strange outward-facing parody of ring-a-ring-a'-roses. Then she makes us tilt our heads so we're all looking 'up at the glass, *properly*, Mum,' and then we're turning faster and faster until we are all, all three of us, dizzy and laughing as black clouds tumble across the sky, and the rain starts to pelt down above our heads and drums out a tune I could never sing . . .

But the moment is spoiled when Isa declares in a loud, excited voice: 'Look, that pigeon's just pooped on the glass!'

She pulls her hand away from mine to point it out, but she keeps her other one in Scott's, and he keeps his in mine, and then he laughs and looks at where she's pointing.

I don't want to be the first one to relax my grip, which throws me somewhat. But eventually I do, because let's face it, it would just be ultra-weird if I held his hand for any length of time, given our verbal spats and history.

It sort of marks a turning point, though, that strange little game. And I understand for certain that Isa will suddenly know that she has free range around the building, and neither of us will ever do anything to stop it.

## Scott

While I'd never say Liza and I had become the best of friends after 'The Moment' under the pyramid, we've turned a corner, I think. There's some sort of guarded truce in place and we can almost stick to it.

By that, I mean we can occasionally be in the same room as one another and not want to claw each other's eyes out. She's got very nice eyes, to be honest. Almond-shaped and dark brown. Really long lashes. Not that I've made a concentrated study of them. They remind me too much of another pair of dark brown eyes, the sort of dark brown eyes that, once upon a time, and yes, maybe once again, I could get lost in.

But regardless, Liza seems to like her kitchen area, and she's busy sorting out a colour scheme for the rest of the place. The units she has are quite vintage and country kitchen. I can see it working if she aims for a fusion of shabby chic and kitsch — chintz and gingham and jam jars full of fresh meadow flowers. Tiny milk-churns and mismatched china. You know the sort of thing I mean.

But I'm staying out of it. The bottom floor is her dream, not mine.

'Mum's getting a delivery today,' Isa tells me as she wanders upstairs to see if I've got an iPad charger. I have, and she squirrels it away in her pocket. I'll have to remember to get it back. It's still raining outside, it's Saturday and her friend Sophie wasn't free, so the kid's a bit bored.

'Is she now, brat?' I ask. I hoist myself up on my kitchen unit and reach for a chair so I can plant my feet on it.

'Yeah.' Isa hoists herself up onto my desk, which is now not-so makeshift, but I don't complain. So long as she doesn't knock anything off it. She plants her feet on my desk chair. I reach behind me and find an opened packet of KitKats.

I toss one across the gap and she catches it deftly. 'She says it's a load of stuff she got at the auction on Tuesday.' She slits the silver paper with a short fingernail, sparkly pink nail varnish flakes notwithstanding. 'She says there's a piano in it.'

'A piano?' I'm a bit stunned. Liza

doesn't strike me as musical.

'Yes. She says it'll fill in the gap by the stairs. I think she wants to paint it white and stencil flowers on it.' Isa pulls a face and I see she doesn't like the idea of a flowery, white piano. 'I'd like it just left . . . normal. You know. Like wood coloured.' She devours the first finger of the KitKat. 'She says if it looks crap, she can use it as a bookcase or put flowers in the top and make a water feature of it in the courtyard. With a waterfall coming out and over the keys.' She looks at me, indignantly.

'Oh.' I'm not sure if I'm more thrown by Liza's ideas for a piano or Isa's use of the word 'crap'.

'Pinterest,' says Isa, rather disgustedly. 'She pokes around on it all the time.'

'Ah.'

'I like looking at tattoos on it,' she offers, more brightly.

'Okay. Do you . . . want . . . a tattoo then?' I ask.

'Yeah. When I'm older. I want a rose.

Or a skull. Can't decide. Might get an angel.' She polishes off the second finger of the KitKat and jumps down from the desk. 'I'll get one when I'm eighteen. See you later.' She bounds off across the room and I stare after her.

A tattoo.

Well now.

I wonder if her mother knows?

Just then, there's the hiss of an air-brake outside, followed by the *beep-beep-beep* of a reversing lorry. This must be the piano, then.

This I have to see.

# 8

## Liza

'This way!' I cry, stepping over paint equipment, Scott's toolbox (which I borrowed to put some shelves up) and Isa, who seems to be everywhere today, like a rash. 'Over here.'

Two guys. who look the spit of Laurel and Hardy *hurumph*, grunt, groan and break wind heartily as they waddle across the pavement with the intention, I hope, of bringing the piano home to roost.

'In the corner, hen?' asks Laurel.

'Under the stairs,' I tell him.

'Aye,' he says and stumbles towards the door. 'Door might have to come off. Aye.'

I put my hands on my head and watch them, praying they'll make it safely and won't dismantle my new door; the new door that swings to and fro perfectly and has a little bell that goes *ding* when someone opens it. Without really realising I'm doing it, I scrunch up two handfuls of hair and tug at them in worry.

'A piano. Intriguing.'

I turn, and he's leaning against the wall, arms folded, one leg bent up behind him, smirking.

'Yes,' I snap. I drop my arms to my side, and he flicks a glance at my hair which must look like a ginger furze bush.

He reaches out and, quite gently, smooths down first one side then the other. It generates one of those odd, zingy *twangs* again and my soul batters deep within my heart, threatening to break free. I ignore it. 'Not a professional look,' he says and refolds his arms.

'Don't care,' I snap again. 'I just want the stuff in there and it's ridiculous. Look at them!' They've literally just crunched into the corner of the door frame.

'Whoopsy daisy,' chortles Hardy, and stumbles on the step.

I compress my lips and stare at them.

'It's best not to look,' says Scott. 'Come on. Let's end the misery and get the rest of the stuff.'

He pushes himself away from the wall and takes a couple of long strides towards the lorry. He turns and points inside. 'You want to tell me what's yours?'

I join him and peer inside the gloomy, sweaty-smelling depths. 'All of it,' I say after looking at the boxes.

'All of it?'

I can tell he's not that impressed. 'Yes,' I say sharply. 'Books, paintings, antiques. They're all there. And I've got some more crockery and stuff for the tea-shop. It's going to be vintage kitsch. Shabby chic. You know?'

He smiles into the darkness of the lorry. 'I do know. Okay. Let's start. Brat! Over here please!'

Isa runs over from where she's been watching the farce. She doesn't object to the fact he calls her 'brat', but if anyone called her a 'spoiled brat', for instance, she would go ape. I know this from experience.

'What shall I take?' she asks.

'These books. Can you manage?'

'Yeah.' She takes an armful of books then stands and looks at the men, who have just managed to manoeuvre the piano in. 'I like it wood coloured,' she says, rather sadly. Then she hurries in after them, and I shake my head. It'll get painted white. It damn well will.

'Just anywhere?' Scott asks as he lifts a box effortlessly. He's not wearing a jacket and I can see his biceps tense attractively as he clutches the box.

For a moment, I'm thrown, but I tear my gaze away and grab a box of paintings. 'Just anywhere.'

'Cool.'

It's an echo of Isa, and I wonder briefly if he's been spending too much time with her and she's rubbing off on him.

'There are soft furnishings as well,' I

say, to dull the idea of the similarities between them. 'Cushions. Lots of cushions. And some pashminas.'

'Pash-bloody-minas?' he says. 'What for?'

'People like them!' I say, defending my choice of stock. 'And those, and the cushions are over-stock from another gift shop. They can find a home here.'

'Okay,' he says, but he still doesn't sound convinced.

Well he's a bloke, so what does he know?

'It's my shop!'

'Okay.' He half-smiles. 'That's cool. But if they *are* over-stock from a local gift shop, what does that tell you?'

I'm silent. I don't really know.

'It means,' he says, 'that local gift shops can't sell them. So you might have a job to shift them too.' He shrugs his broad shoulders and grins, almost apologetically. 'Just saying. It'll be fine if you got them on sale or return though, I'm sure.'

You see, I didn't do that at all.

Not sale or return.

At all.

And now I'm a bit worried.

'Well — just don't bloody *bother* saying,' I growl, for want of anything better to say myself. I stomp past him with my paintings.

If I want to sell pashminas and cushions, I'll jolly well sell pashminas and cushions.

I bet there's a market for them, anyway, far away from Scott up-his-own-backside McCreadie.

I just *bet* there is.

## Scott

She's never going to sell those pashminas. Or the cushions.

Never.

Ever.

But what the hell do I know? I'm just a bloke.

107

# 9

## Liza

Isa is pounding on the keys, her face screwed up in concentration. She's been mithering on to play that damn piano for weeks. She did try to hide my paint pots and stencils, but I found them in Scott's workshop cupboard, and she was told that because of that, she could not, under any circumstances, play on it. Ever. At all.

Which she didn't take any notice of whatsoever.

'For God's sake!' I snap, exasperated. 'Either play a proper tune or stop it.'

'I want keyboard lessons,' demands my daughter, the future Elton John. 'And this is as close as I can *get*.'

'A piano is *not* a keyboard,' I reply, then wonder if that's a contradiction in terms.

'It *is*,' she replies and hammers out another rendition of 'Chopsticks'. I've got to hand it to her, it doesn't sound too bad — Sophie played it in a school concert and Isa was determined to master the awful tune too. I just wish she'd play something different.

Isa pauses and starts testing out keys for 'Jingle Bells', and I grit my teeth as I really do not want to think about Christmas. She moves onto 'Silent Night', which is just as bad for my nerves.

'That's a truly terrible noise.'

I turn and see Scott lounging against the door frame. He's laughing and looking at Isa. I want to agree with him, but I don't, on principle. He said he didn't like the fact I'd painted the piano and hates the stencilled flowers on it, and I suspect he helped my daughter hide my equipment, but what does he know? He's not The Edge from U2 or Rick Wakeman or a famous pianist at all. Not even — thank God, because I can't imagine Scott in spangles — Liberace.

I dip my paintbrush into the pot and attack the wall again. 'She's doing no harm.'

'She's doing no music, either. Come on, brat.' He pushes himself away from the door frame and saunters across to the piano.

'Don't you need to be busy upstairs instead of encouraging her?' I ask, icily.

'Nope.'

I glance over and see Isa turn her screwed-up face towards him.

'I bet you can't play,' she fires at him.

'Bet I can,' he fires back. 'Shift.'

She shuffles, apparently under sufferance, along the piano seat and makes room for him.

'Okay. Try this.' He presses some keys and a tune comes out. 'Can you repeat that?'

'Of course,' she says, sniffing arrogantly. And she repeats it perfectly.

'Awesome. Try this.'

So she does, and gets it spot on.

Scott nods. 'Now try putting them together.' He demonstrates and Isa watches intently.

It's Isa's turn to nod, and she puts them together as she's instructed.

'Fantastic. Now — you do that again, and I'll add some melody.'

Isa pauses, and sticks her tongue out between her teeth. She peers at the keys and picks out the tune. Scott joins in and I almost drop my paintbrush. I recognise the tune.

''The Dance of the Sugar Plum Fairy'!' I say. 'God, that's actually quite good.'

A smile twitches at the side of Scott's mouth. 'Again, brat,' he says. 'You can do better than that, surely.'

'It's easy!' she snaps and pounds out her half of the tune again, faultlessly. Scott jumps in and they finish on a flourish.

'Again!' cries Isa. She's actually smiling, and she even looks just like him, with that same evil grin. Like they're in cahoots. 'I want it perfect. I want to play better than Sophie.'

'You can do a duet with Sophie, can't

you? Teach her what to do?'

'No! No. I'm not letting her near it.' She starts hammering out the tune again and Scott joins in to help her.

'I think that's enough, Isa,' I say. 'You've proved yourself.'

'I *like* it,' she growls, and off they go again.

I think I'm going to grow to hate this tune.

I think I wish I had some earplugs.


## Scott

I smile to myself and play the tune again and again, largely to annoy Liza, but also because the brat seems to be enjoying it.

'Do you like the piano?' I ask her.

She nods. 'Yeah. But I can't learn it properly. I just know bits.'

'I used to play this tune with my brother Billy,' I tell her. 'The rest of my brothers and my sister aren't that good with music. We were the ones who stuck at our lessons. We had a band at one point.'

'I'm going to be in a rock band,' Isa informs me.

'Cool,' I say. 'Nothing wrong with a bit of ambition.'

'I sing as well,' she informs me. 'So, I can play the guitar and sing along like Jared Leto or Matt Bellamy.'

I'm impressed. 'Certainly not bad ambitions to have,' I agree. 'It takes a lot of work though. And practice. Loads of practice.'

'I'd be able to practice more if I had a piano at home. My guitar is okay, because it doesn't take up much room. But a piano . . . ' She sighs, lustily.

'You're not getting a piano,' chips in Liza, without even turning her head. She stabs at a corner of the wall angrily, splaying the bristles of the brush, blobby paint running down the freshly coloured wall. 'The flat is not big enough. You can use this one if you have to.'

Isa rolls her eyes and bashes both

hands on the keys. 'It's not *fair*,' she grumbles, and I dip my head so she doesn't see me smirking. It's so exactly what Nessa was like at that age.

'It's the way it is,' mutters Liza dangerously.

'We are where we are,' says Isa in a sarcastic, sing-song voice. I think it must be something she's heard before and wasn't impressed with then, either.

'Isa — ' snaps Liza, throwing her brush down with a soggy *slap*.

'Come on,' I say. 'Enough. What's the problem, brat? You can use this one like your mum says.'

'But only when she's here. I'm not allowed here on my own.'

'That's only right,' I reply. 'She probably doesn't trust an unleashed brat.'

'You're just as *bad*!' she moans and stomps off towards the courtyard.

'Yeah, I never said I was any good with kids.' I watch the kid in question disappear outside, where she throws herself into the swing, facing pointedly

114

away from the open doors. 'She's probably annoyed that she couldn't slam them.'

'More than likely,' replies Liza. 'But I hate the smell of paint fumes so they're staying open.'

I pick out a few notes on the piano, and then, getting into it, I play the first few bars of one of my favourite songs.

'"Bohemian Rhapsody"! Now you're showing off.'

I don't deny it. It always sounds quite impressive. I give it full throttle for a few minutes and then finish up. I've missed playing the piano I realise, and it's nice to get back into it. Before I can stop myself, I hear myself make an offer. 'I don't mind teaching Isa a bit, you know. We can use this thing.' I run my hands over the keys. 'It's a bit old, and to be honest it looks shit painted white, and it's a bit out of tune in one or two spots, but I can easily fix that. In fact — '

' — Get *out* of my piano,' snarls Liza. 'God knows what you're doing in there.'

I ignore her and continue to poke around amongst the strings. I twiddle a couple of the tuning pegs. 'That should do it,' I say and press the dodgy keys again. 'Perfect. If the kid wants to play the thing, you should let her. If she's got an interest in it, and she sticks at it, it'll keep her mind off boys in the future.'

'Ha!' Liza folds her arms and glares at me. 'And did it keep your mind off girls?' Her eyes rake me all over, and I feel rather exposed and uncomfortable.

'My reputation must precede me,' I say and try to charm her with a McCreadie Smile. My music attracted them more, now I think about it. So yes. I should know better. And funnily enough, I don't want Liza judging me on my past.

Liza turns away, unmoved, and picks up her paintbrush again, stabbing it into the paint. The colour is drying all streaky on the wall and I daren't tell her it looks like she's missed a bit in the corner.

'No. I just think I know your type rather too well,' she says, viciously poking at a spot she's already poked at. 'Musicians and stuff. We'll see about the lessons.' She purses her lips and I feel the conversation has ended. I shrug and move away.

'No problem. Okay. I'm heading back upstairs. I just came down to see what the noise was.' I pause for a second, perhaps to appreciate her bum in her soft, pale pink jogging bottoms, then I speak again. 'I've just boiled the kettle. D'you want anything?'

'No thank you,' she says, and doesn't bother turning back to me.

Not that I feel offended by that. Not at all.

I wouldn't take a cuppa she'd offered me.

It would probably be a poisoned chalice, knowing Liza-Belle Graham.

So, I head upstairs and set the kettle to boil again. It wasn't a lie. I had boiled it, and then I got distracted by 'Chopsticks'. I gaze out of the window idly while I'm waiting for the tea to stew, and watch Isa swing back and forwards, back and forwards. Her face is set stonily, and she reminds me even more of my sister.

I think I might take my mug of tea outside into the courtyard. It's a nice enough day, and I could do with some fresh air.

I might have taken a few chocolate biscuits out with me. And I might have taken a bottle of Pepsi out there too — I just happened to have it in the fridge.

'We meet again, brat,' I say, and sit on the edge of a raised stone flower bed. I think it'll be nice to maybe make a sensory garden out here for people to enjoy when Liza's pie-in-the-sky tea-shop opens.

'Yeah? And?' Isa glares at me and I nod. Definitely Nessa.

'And. I just wondered if you wanted piano lessons?' I toss the bottle to her, and when she's caught it, I toss one, two, three biscuits over too. By the time she's caught the third biscuit, she's actually grinning.

'Thanks. Yes. I *do* want piano lessons, but Mum isn't keen.' She does an eye-roll that would make a teenager proud. 'They cost too much and she says I won't keep it up.' She compresses her lips into a thin little line, then clearly realises she can't eat or drink like that, so she uncompresses them and nibbles at a biscuit. 'But you know what, I *do* sing as well. I'm really quite good. Like I told you, I want to be like Jared Leto or Matt Bellamy, and I bet *they* were allowed lessons.'

'If you learned to play the piano, you could be like Elton John as well,' I tell her.

Isa looks at me blankly. I guess he's not on her radar that much.

'Who?' she asks.

'An old bloke. Forget it,' I say. Engaging with children isn't my strong point.

'Oh.'

'Gary Barlow?' I try. 'Not so old

bloke. Sings and plays piano?'

There's a flicker of recognition. 'There are some dogs that sing and play piano on YouTube,' she comments, opening the bottle of Pepsi with a *fizz*.

'Are you supposed to be watching YouTube at your age?' I ask.

She looks at me as if I'm stupid, then shakes her head at my idiocy. She isn't going to elaborate.

A smile twitches at the side of my mouth despite her apparent opinion of me. 'Okay. Well, just so you know, I've offered to teach you piano. You might have to convince your mum a bit, but I think we'll be okay on the one in there.' I nod to the building.

'It's out of tune, though. We need to sort that out first,' she tells me.

'Already sorted,' I reply.

She looks up at me, properly, and her green eyes glint with mischief.

'Then *cheers*,' she says, and raises her bottle.

I pause for only a millisecond and grin back. 'Cheers to you too.'

I clink my cup against her bottle, and she laughs. 'I know where the key is anyway. I pinched the spare one, but don't tell Mum.' She leans to one side and fishes inside her pocket. 'See? That means I can use the piano any time I like, so I can practise, can't I?'

Isa tucks the key back in her pocket, and I wonder if I *should* tell Liza. I glance at the shop. But then, what harm can Isa do, really? I'm here a lot of the time anyway, and I doubt she'll be given *that* much freedom at this age, so she's not going to be wandering around on her own. I put the notion out of my head. I'll just remember to expect a ten-year-old girl instead of musical burglars who can't resist a rendition of 'Chopsticks', if I ever hear anything like that downstairs.

But that sort of reminds me of something I also have to say. 'Oh — the first thing I'm going to teach you is some Black Sabbath or David Bowie.' I shake my head gravely. 'I can't tolerate 'Chopsticks' any longer. You need to know some decent stuff. It'll hold your interest more.'

'Deal!' she says. 'I can't tolerate bloody 'Chopsticks' any longer myself.'

I don't tell her off for swearing. I'm too busy biting my lip and trying not to laugh.

# 10

## Scott

I pull up to the side of Phoenix Antiques in the van and see a child lounging against the front door. The child has long, red hair and is inspecting a green sparkly nail today. The child is also wearing a school uniform.

'And the reason you're here is?' I ask as I approach her.

'I've come for my first piano lesson.'

'Oh. And does your mother know?'

'Yes.' She looks me directly in the eyes and nods. 'Yes, she does.'

'Do I need to contact said mother to check?'

'No. No you don't. She was going to send me with a note, but I said there was no need because you'd said you would do it and you'd offered and stuff.'

I shrug. 'Okay. Well, I can give you half an hour, then I'll need to do some work.'

'That's fine. I can get the bus home afterwards. It's only three stops. I counted.'

'No, you can't. I'll drop you off.'

'Yes, I can. I get it to school. It's the same bus — but in the other direction. I know exactly where I'm going.' She compresses her lips and folds her arms. 'I get the bus every day and it's not an issue. It's a perfectly acceptable thing to do. When I have after-school clubs I get the bus home. The drivers all know me and watch out for me. It'll be Jock today as it's Tuesday.'

I shake my head. My heart is screaming 'Nessa!' and I'd rather not look at Isa, for fear I start seeing more similarities.

Instead, I rummage in my pocket for the key and open up. Isa waits patiently, watching me while I unset the intruder alarm and then following me to the piano.

124

She pulls a face. 'I really don't like it white and flowery.' She hops onto the seat and lifts the lid. She runs her fingers avariciously along the keys and tests the couple that were out of tune at the weekend. 'Perfect.'

'Glad you approve,' I say. 'Now. Any idea what you want to learn? I'm all new to this teaching lark, but as I say we've got half an hour. I'm guessing you don't want to warm up with some scales?'

The disgust in her face at that idea must mirror mine at the idea of wasting good playing time on deathly-dull scales.

'Do I *look* like I need to do scales?' Isa asks and bashes out some pop tune from the latest boy-band.

'That doesn't seem like your kind of music,' I say, frowning at her.

'It's not. I can't abide it. But it's easy to remember. They all use the same combination of chords anyway. Listen.'

She plays a couple more tunes from two other pop groups, and I nod. 'Well done. Vile music, but well done.'

'Thanks.' She puts her hands in her lap and looks at me. 'So. Black Sabbath? Or David Bowie?'

'Queen. 'Bohemian Rhapsody'. It's a rite of passage. You learn that, you impress a *lot* of people.'

'I want to be impressive,' she acknowledges, with a little nod of her head.

'And so you shall be,' I say. 'Budge along, brat. This is how it starts.'

And we spend the next half hour, heads bent over the piano, learning and teaching 'Bohemian Rhapsody'.

It's a lot of fun.

And she's pretty damn impressive by the end of it.

## Liza

It's about two weeks until I think we'll be ready for opening and it's getting quite exciting. Isa is coming along with me quite happily to Phoenix Antiques

— although that might be because she's absolutely obsessed with that piano.

She's really getting good at it, despite the fact she still moans about it being white. But so what? I saw it done on Pinterest and I was determined to do it as well. And I know Isa's got an innate talent anyway — so much for Scott offering lessons. Like she really needs them!

I allow myself a moment of pride. Then there's a little stab of regret that her father will probably never hear her playing, and it's such a shame. Still — we can manage fine. We can, and we do.

I haven't seen Scott for a few weeks. It's good and it's bad. He's been sorting things out in Glasgow every weekend. As I understand it, he's still got a flat over there, so he's been staying away from a Wednesday night to a Monday afternoon. He's back here Tuesdays and Wednesdays, but that's it for the minute, and I'm at the vet's those days so don't see him.

He didn't even tell me in person that he was going. I got a note, which was fine. It was stuck under a milk-jug shaped like a cow, which he knows is Isa's favourite bit of tat in the whole place.

In the note he said that his part of Phoenix is more or less good to go, and he's temporarily moved west to pick up that side of things. He says it's a way to let me finish off my part of Phoenix uninterrupted, but if I need anything, I just have to let him know. And he's left his tool-box at the bottom of the stairs along with some picture hooks, if I need them at all.

He says expanding his interior design business is like juggling, and he's got to keep all the balls in the air. He's worried he's let the Glasgow one slide a bit because he's been sorting Edinburgh out.

I can't even imagine having more than one premises. One is enough for me, and I know how very, very lucky I am to have it.

Even if I have to share it with Scott McCreadie.

Although I do think I sort of miss him lurking in the shadows like an even darker shadow, his face a pale oval, his eyes darker still, that fringe flopping over one of them. When he emerges, he sort of melts out of the darkness, I've noticed, and he's smiling more and scowling less these days, so it's nice. But the more I get to know him, to get to know what he's *really* like, the more I'm feeling that tug of wanting to be near him. Which isn't exactly the sensible option, and I've run away from relationships for less than that — before, obviously, I had Isa to tie me down and keep me in one place.

'There's no note today,' says Isa, checking underneath the cow. 'Will he be back the weekend after next? Because that's before we open, isn't it?' She turns the cow-jug over in her hand thoughtfully.

'I guess he'll be back by then,' I say. 'Do you miss him?'

'Me? Oh, no,' says Isa. She puts the cow on the piano. 'I'll see him when he's around. Can I go and play on the swing?'

I smile and nod. 'Yes. Get yourself out there. Once we open, you'll be chasing little kids off it, so you might as well enjoy yourself. I want to make sure the toilets have got everything in them.' I've got little wicker baskets all ready to fill with tissues and cotton wool balls. There's a selection of pretty hand-washes and moisturisers, and a big rose-entwined heart to hang on the door of the ladies'.

I'm not sure what to put on the men's, but Isa suggested a guitar so it might be an idea. It's that or an anchor. I'll have to speak to Scott and see what —

Then I shake my head. I don't have to speak to Scott at all. It's got nothing to do with him. It's my business. My 'arty-farty-crafty-dafty shop', as he called it last month.

It's mine.

*So there, Scott. What do I need your opinion for?*

But still — it would be nice to see what he thinks.

I hope he's back next week.

# 11

## Scott

I saunter around the corner, musing at the fact that we've got approximately a week until we open properly.

I've just had a very late lunch at The Witchery on the Royal Mile with Logan from the Glasgow office, and declined his offer of a lift back to the new shop. There was some crisis with a re-claimed fireplace that I'd sourced for a client, and we needed to get it sorted; Logan came over here to help. But now it's all sorted and I'm heading back.

Also, on a more selfish note, I don't want any of the guys to see Phoenix before our grand opening. Anyway, I know Isa will probably be waiting outside the building for me, like she usually does on a Tuesday after school.

Phoenix Antiques is looking pretty

good now. Liza has all her bits and pieces laid out, and I've got the sample books and things upstairs, along with a nice seating area to meet my clients in. I'm going to be working on a tailored appointment basis here, as it's not really big enough for people off the street to wander around randomly. But never mind. 'We are where we are', as someone, quite small and arrogant, once said to me.

And at least there's a tea-shop on site at my new premises — sort of. It's a selling point for a lot of people. I think Liza's hope is that they'll see me, come downstairs for a cuppa and have to walk through her shop to get there. At that point, they'll be thoroughly inspired by my good self to re-do their homes, and they might decide to buy things from Liza. Or they might come back another day, when the work's done. I'll have to have follow-up appointments, of course. Maybe I can chuck in a free pashmina with every consultation, because there's no way she's going to sell them all. She bought dozens of the damn things.

I grin at the thought, then raise my head and sniff the air. There's a strange smell. I look around me and see a plume of smoke rising from a couple of streets away, and I swallow a silly sense of panic.

Just because the plume of smoke coupled with the smell of fire and yes, now I hear it, the crackle of flames, *seem* to be coming from Phoenix Antiques, doesn't necessarily mean that Phoenix Antiques is on fire.

But just in case, I hurry; and then my hurrying turns into jogging; and then my jogging turns into a full-on sprint as something furry comes flying at me, all black spikes and white teeth.

'Mow *wow*!' shrieks Schubert. 'Mow *wow*!' He pelts off and the sense of panic no longer seems silly.

I round the corner and glimpse Liza's red hair, and Nessa's dark hair looking wilder than ever. I push through a crowd of passers-by, who have clearly come to gawp and shout unhelpful things like 'has someone called 999?' instead of actually *ringing* 999, and force myself closer to them, as Schubert growls and hisses at the spectators' feet, making them part like the Red Sea for me. The girls are standing, huddled together outside the building.

'What's happened?' I cry.

My sister turns to me and shakes her head. 'We don't know. I was coming to do a pre-opening landlord check sort of thing on behalf of Mr Hogarth and when Schubert and I arrived here, we saw some smoke coming out of the building. Schubert was quite insistent that I called the fire brigade, and then I called Liza, and she's just turned up. Thank God nobody's in there.'

'Where's Isa?' I ask, sharply, looking around in a panic. 'Where is she?'

'At her after-school club, thank God,' Liza tells me, her brown eyes round with horror. 'It's drama tonight. Then she's going home with Sophie for tea. I just dashed out, I haven't even called

Sophie's mum to warn her I'll be late in because I don't want the bairn going home to an empty house . . . ' Her voice catches and someone close to us shouts as a tongue of fire bursts out of one of the top windows. Illuminated behind it, I can see my units being swallowed up by red and orange flames, licking their way up the walls. The smell of smoke and heat is overpowering, and I run my hand over my face, sweat beading on my skin and my heart pounding. The buildings next to us haven't been touched yet, the fire seems to be contained within our premises for now. In the distance, I hear the sirens telling us that the fire brigade are on their way.

'But Isa,' I repeat. 'Isabel — '

'Mow wow!' screeches Schubert again, and suddenly he launches himself forwards and runs towards the burning building.

'Schubert!' screams Nessa and dives after her cat as he whooshes past her. She makes a pretty good rugby tackle, but his tail slips through her fingers like it's greased with butter.

Then the molten penny drops with a sickening thud, the likes of which I've never felt before: 'Drama?' I stare at Liza, and suddenly all the pieces fit together. 'Tea with Sophie? But it's Tuesday.'

'Yes. She always does that on a Tuesday,' says Liza, her face red and tear-stained as her dream burns in front of us, as if she's challenging me to say she's lying.

'Bloody hell. No she *doesn't*,' I shout. 'She's been coming to see *me* on a Tuesday to have piano lessons! She said you knew all about it. Good God!' I look back at the building, just in time to see Schubert disappear through the door. 'We *always* have our lessons on a Tuesday! She's in there now. She's bloody *in* there!'

## Liza

'She's in there? Isa!' There's a rushing sound in my ears and I start to move

137

forwards, but someone grabs me and thrusts me behind them.

'Stay here. I'm going in,' says Scott. I realise he was the one who grabbed me, and in an instant, he's pulled off his black T-shirt and wrapped it around his face.

Nessa comes running back to us, eyes wide and terrified, horribly Schubert-less. 'Scotty!' she cries as he races past her. 'Oh Scotty!'

'Isa!' I scream, while Nessa hangs onto me, white-faced. 'Scott!' I can't even think about how long this has been going on, about how they've both been going along with it merrily, about how, if Scott hadn't come around that corner when he did —

'They'll be fine. They'll be fine,' says Nessa. 'Schubert . . . ' But even she can't say any more and her fingers dig into my arm.

As Scott disappears into the smoke, something registers in my subconscious and it jerks into the forefront of my brain.

He's got a huge tattoo on his back.

It's a skull with wings coming out of the sides and roses all around it.

The rushing sound comes again and almost deafens me.

# 12

## Scott

Isa must have decided to let herself in. I blame myself. We were at a really complicated bit in a Coldplay song, and she lost her temper with it last week, said she wanted to get some practice in.

And she had a key. She *has* a key. And she's in there. She's learned the alarm code from me — every time those bright, intelligent eyes watched me, she was memorising the number.

I don't think of anything else beyond getting in that building and getting that child out.

I almost trip over Schubert as he prances and jumps around, *mow wow* — ing for all his worth as he, in his own way, directs me through debris and smoke. He knows where she is; I just have to trust him.

Kids can get themselves in all sorts of places during fires. There are nooks and crannies aplenty in this old building. I might have hoped she'd run out of the back door, but for all I know she could have locked herself in the toilets.

I feel sick and duck as something tumbles down near me. I risk looking up and along into the tea-shop, but it's just a wall of flame. There's no way I can get through it. If she's in there — *please God and all the other angels* — I can't do it. I can't do it.

'*Mow wow!*' yells Schubert and draws to a halt by the piano. The cow-jug is on the top and Schubert jumps around, pawing and pointing at the instrument. He pounces once, twice, three times, then gets behind me. '*Mow wow!*'

I lean down and my heart somer-saults. *Thank you, thank you.*

'Come on,' I say, throwing myself

down next to the little girl. Schubert runs away, clearly having done his job and I know, somehow, he'll make it safely outside. The smoke is choking me and my eyes are stinging, even through the shirt. 'Come on, brat. Get up.'

Isa looks really tiny in her school uniform, all curled up underneath the piano and coughing, struggling for breath through the acrid smoke. She's trapped under there by one of the shelving units that's fallen down, but I think she's tried to make a run for it before that. The piano stool has toppled over — I guess she's tripped up because there's blood on her forehead where she's maybe whacked it on the unit as she's fallen. It was the ridiculous pashmina display on those shelves, and all the fabric is shrivelling and burning up around her . . .

Around her.

Around her in a perfect circle.

She's right in the centre of it, like she's being protected by flaming

142

swords. And, somehow, I'm in the middle of it with her.

But she's not answering me, and my heart begins to pound. This is like my worst nightmare — I thought it was bad enough seeing bloody Schubert run in here, but this is a million times worse.

'Sorry, little one. I can't let you stay here. Even though your mum is going to kill us both anyway.'

I take a couple of breaths, then rip the shirt off my face, and somehow pick her up, snuggle her in and chuck the fabric over her nose and mouth. I make a grab for the cow-jug, lean my head down, bury my own nose in my shirt and start to retrace my steps. There's a creak and a crack and I know that sound — it's the triangular glass structure upstairs breaking and the staircase crumbling away.

I swear to myself, but angels or demons, I'm not sure which, lend speed to me and I rush through the wall of flames towards the door with Isa before we get showered with glass shards.

143

I'm shaking and I think I'm going to pass out. This is far too much to cope with. One of these things alone would have been intolerable, never mind three of them together: my daughter, my potential business, my daughter's father. Her *father*?

The thought sends me crumpling to my knees, the world going in and out of focus.

'How? *How*?' I repeat. Something is kneading my shoulders and I realise it's Nessa rubbing them. And there's a heavy weight in my lap. Schubert's head lies there like a hot boulder, his eyes fixed on mine.

Automatically, my hand strays to his black, furry head and he closes his eyes in ecstasy as I mirror Nessa's movements.

'She must have been waiting for him,' says Nessa, thinking I mean 'how is Isa in there?' 'She must have a key.'

I shake my head. 'No. I mean, *how*?

How is it *him*? Why didn't I *know*?'

'Know what?'

'That it's him. Isa's father. It's *him*.' My head starts to pound and, even though I'm on the ground already, I think I'm truly going to pass out and fall forward.

'Scotty? Well, yes — '

But Nessa's words are interrupted by the fire engine sirens blaring even more loudly down the road, and a shout from a random passer-by: 'Look! Look! He's got a little girl!'

I force myself to stay conscious and focus on the door. Sure enough, there's a figure coming out, pursued by flames and smoke — and it *is* just like something out of a Meat Loaf music video. Ironically, I think of that first altercation in the courtyard. Why didn't I realise then? Before then? At the bar! I was centimetres from his face; it was his eyes. I should have remembered his eyes if nothing else — his scent — woodsmoke and spice — his touch, his lips . . . everything. But I did, didn't

145

I? Subconsciously at least. That's why I've been thinking of him, and that night, more and more and more — and wondering, Lord help me, what Fate was playing at.

'Oh God!' I scramble to my feet, Schubert *flumph*-ing off to one side as he rolls away from my lap looking slightly startled, his legs sticking straight out, unbending. I run towards Scott. He's got my daughter — our daughter — in his arms and she's coughing and gasping, which is a good sign, right? 'Isa! Isabel! Isabel!' I cry and he hands her over wordlessly. They both smell of smoke and there's another siren coming now — an ambulance, I realise, vaguely.

I hold Isa tightly and my tears fall onto her hot, red little face. 'Thank you. Thank you,' I whisper. Scott embraces us both, and his head dips briefly so his forehead is touching mine. His arms feel strong and safe and whatever has or has not happened between us over the last ten years

146

means nothing, nothing at all. All that matters is that my little girl is safe and in my arms. I don't care about Phoenix Antiques burning to the ground in front of us. I don't care about anything else.

'Mummy?' Isa asks in a small, cracked voice. 'I'm sorry. I'm sorry.'

'Don't be sorry, Isa. Don't be sorry,' I sob.

I hold her close and hug her until the paramedics come and lead us to the ambulance. I don't know at what point Scott let us go, but I look back towards where we were standing, and Nessa is hugging him, Schubert is winding himself around his legs, but Scott is just staring at me and Isa, his arms wrapped around his body as another paramedic wraps a blanket around his shoulders.

The paramedic says something, and Scott, still staring at us, shakes his head imperceptibly. He's got something in his hand. The cow-jug. He's holding it like a talisman.

Nessa punches him lightly on the arm. 'Yes,' she says. 'Of course he wants to go to the hospital with them. He's her father. He's simply in shock.'

# 13

## Scott

I'm not sure at which point I realised. I think, subconsciously, I'd known since the first moment I saw her.

I had sort of recognised Liza in the pub. It was the way she moved, the way she giggled as she stumbled over the chair leg, and that stupid, but adorable comment she'd made about it being the chair's fault. I knew that I had to get talking to her, that night in the pub, because the memories were rushing in and almost drowning me. I thought I'd buried that night a long time ago, when I believed there was never going to be a chance of seeing her again.

My dark side won when I first met her; I did what I — what we both — wanted to do, and to hell with the consequences. I swooped in and we took each other in a way that had never happened before or since. It was as if we had finally found what we needed in one another and the memory of it has haunted me ever since.

I'm not sure why she left in such a hurry, with such a strange choice of words that burned themselves into my dark old soul.

I'm not sure why I didn't follow her across the river, because I should have done.

But the night I saw her in that pub, I had a flashback to that time, eleven years ago, when someone had stumbled over my guitar.

I'd had way too much to drink — I wasn't even supposed to be there. My friend Davy, a post-graduate student, lived in the flat, and I was passing through on my way to conquer Glasgow. Davy had suggested a drink before I went home, and one drink had turned into too many, as it can do when you're young and stupid. I knew there was no way I was getting anywhere else that night, so I just kept drinking.

I'd met Liza in the fifth bar — she'd been dancing on the table, and I had joined her. We'd eventually climbed down, laughing. She'd aimed a kiss at me, and I caught it. Then we had woven our way to the bar, had more to drink, then reeled back to Davy's flat. God knows where Davy had gone.

One thing had led to another, and the next couple of hours were filled with warm bodies, tangled kisses and soft touches. Then she'd left and fell over the guitar on her way. I'd dropped to my knees and tried to grab her leg, seeing she'd injured herself on the coffee table, but she laughed again and flipped her hair away from her face as she'd looked down at me.

'It's nothing,' she'd said.

'It's bleeding,' I'd said, feeling the warm, sticky liquid on my fingertips, smelling the faint iron tang. 'But I'm pretty sure the table was at fault.'

'Not bleeding much. And it was. It

was *deferably* at fault. But I feel sorrier for your guitar.'

She'd nodded in its direction, and I saw one of the tuning pegs was hanging off. 'Bloody hell! What did you do to it?' I cried in mock-horror, and she giggled.

I stood up unsteadily and she kissed me. 'I'm sorry. I'm so very sorry.'

'So you should be!' I replied. I wobbled over to my poor instrument and picked it up.

'That's not all I'm sorry about.' Her voice was strange all of a sudden. 'I'm sorry because I have to go and I have to go now, because if I *don't* go, I'll want to stay and that's not what I do.'

'Wait! What?' I turned back, my heart doing a weird pounding thing which it had never done before over a girl, and there was nothing left of her but an open door, a faint trace of perfume and some unsteady clip-clopping steps going down the main staircase. I debated going after her but something stopped me.

Because that wasn't what I did either.

So instead, I propped the guitar back against the wall.

Then I shut the door, my head spinning, intending to go back to bed to sleep it off. But, for once, the better part of me won, and something hidden deep inside me urged me to run to the staircase and follow the red-haired girl.

I raced to the bottom and burst out of the door, and there was nothing to see and nobody to be seen, just the moonlight and starlight glinting off the river that ran behind Davy's flat, and a darker shadow on the other side of the river, with the impression of wild, curly hair that blew out behind her in a wind that didn't exist as she disappeared into the darkness beyond . . .

We didn't even know each other's names.

And I've cursed myself ever since.

And then when I saw Isa in the courtyard; saw her eyes staring into mine with such a challenge, I'd done a double-take. I thought the expression

153

and the attitude were the only things that were familiar, and only because I was so used to that expression and that attitude from within myself. But now I come to think about it, I think it was more than that. I think it was her eyes.

I'd seen those eyes staring back at me in the mirror all my life.

And when she mentioned the swing at Nessa's house — that sealed it, I think. She looked like her, she sounded like her and she was draped with cat — just like her. And Schubert doesn't attach himself to just anyone.

'Scotty?' Nessa presses her fingers into my arm and brings me back to the present. Isa and Liza are in the ambulance. I clear my throat and shake my head. 'They won't want me there,' I say

'You should be there,' says my sister. She leans into me. 'She knows. She knows now, Scotty.'

I blink and shake my head again.

'Over here!' bellows Nessa suddenly, freezing everyone into inaction. 'He's *definitely* in shock. Get him in there with them now please!'

Schubert raises his head and joins in. 'Mow *wow*!' he screeches, in that way that only Schubert can do. 'Mow *wow*!'

'Oh, for God's sake!' I snap, shaking Nessa's grip off me, shoving the cow-jug at her. 'I'll go, okay? Bloody hell. I'll *go*.'

## Liza

It might have been a very awkward journey in the ambulance had we not been staring fixedly at Isa, her face half-hidden by an oxygen mask. We were, quite definitely, *not* staring at each other.

I had one of Isa's hands in mine, and, after a moment, Scott took her other one. He was rubbing her fingers gently with his, and I felt myself wobble with the memory of Isa playing the piano and the guitar, and Scott's capable-looking fingers doing the same. I

155

recalled him showing her how to do that silly 'Sugar Plum Fairy' duet on the piano and I should have known *then*. But hadn't there always been something about him? Something hovering just out of reach that I couldn't quite grab. There was just a sense of . . . *something*.

And now I knew what it was.

I chanced a look at him, and at that very moment he chanced a look at me. I couldn't read the expression in his eyes, but he half-smiled.

'We should probably talk,' he said.

'We probably should,' I replied.

And now there's quite possibly no more 'probably' as we are currently sitting either side of Isa, who looks small and pink in a white hospital bed, her red hair tangled and messy on the pillow. Every so often, she coughs, and one of us helps her to have a drink of water.

Thankfully, she's fine, although she's drifting in and out of sleep at the minute. They said she was suffering a little bit from smoke inhalation, but she's very lucky and not burnt. There's no damage to her lungs, but she'll probably have a sore throat for a few days. She's also sporting a pretty impressive sticking plaster on her forehead where she cut it.

It's a small price to pay.

But we still haven't talked about our Past. Because that's what it's become in my head: our Past, with a capital 'P'. The afternoon has slid by in a blur of uniforms and statements. The police are involved, and we've had to talk to them and we haven't had a minute really — until now.

Until, that is, a nurse walks in and smiles at us. She has a clipboard with her and she's scribbling notes. 'Isabel Graham?' she asks.

'Isa,' I say. 'She prefers to be called Isa.'

'Isa. Lovely. And you're Mum and Dad, yes?'

I open my mouth to deny it, then close it again. Biologically, it's true.

'Yeah.'

I look at Scott in surprise. His voice is strong and confident. There's no denial at all in it. His gaze slides across to me.

I find myself nodding. 'Aye.'

'Super. And Dad — you're the one that pulled her out, is that right?' The nurse doesn't wait for a response. 'What a hero. They're all talking about you out there.' She nods to the bustling corridors beyond the room.

A ghost of a smile flickers across his face. 'I'm not sure if Isa sees me like a hero,' he says. 'I've spent the last few weeks in a battle of wills with her.'

I surprise myself again. 'But you are a hero,' I hear myself say. 'Even if that piano duet absolutely did my head in.'

His smile widens and he looks across at me. 'She does need to practise more.'

'Oh, my daughter hates her music lessons!' says the nurse, moving across to the bed and checking Isa over. 'Mind you, a violin and a seven-year-old should never be put in the same room together.'

She bustles around, chit-chatting about her daughter and the fire and how lucky Isa and Scott are. Isa needs to be kept in for observation overnight, apparently, and Scott could do worse than stay in himself. But he just shakes his head and says he's fine.

There's a knock on the door of the room and we all look up. Nessa is standing there, holding hands with a man who towers over us all. 'Hello,' she says. 'Ewan and I are going to sit with our niece for a little while and let you two go for a coffee.'

'Niece?' I say a little stupidly. Then I shake my head and hold my hands up in the air. 'Of course, of course.' I'm conscious of the nurse still being there, so I simply smile and stand up. Scott stands up too and wipes his hands down his black jeans. He's still wearing the blanket the paramedics gave him.

'I'd love to, but I'm not really dressed

for — ' he starts.

Nessa silences him by producing, with a sort of flourish, a black T-shirt from an enormous bag she's practically dragging along the floor. 'One of my Ewan's T-shirts. Just for you.' She then produces the cow-jug and sets it on the side table. 'The cow-jug is quite safe, I'm pleased to say,' she announces.

Scott glances over at Ewan and nods. 'Thanks, Ewan. I owe you.'

'Don't worry about that,' replies Ewan. 'I'm just pleased you're okay. Both of you.' He looks at the bed and hovers uncertainly in the doorway, attached to Nessa.

'Ewan's been in London,' says Nessa, by way of an explanation. 'I've filled him in on everything, but I had to interrupt the studio meeting with Quentin to do so. But Brad was cool about it. He said he knows what it's like to suddenly have an extended family, so we're fine. We're absolutely fine here. They flew Ewan back as soon as they could so he could be with us.'

*Brad? Quentin?* I look at the wall of muscle that is Nessa's partner and I vaguely remember something about him working in gangster films and Martin Scorsese and Leo di Caprio. Then I swear the enormous bag sort of moves and a black ear pops out of it, flicks around like a furry periscope, and disappears again.

It's too much to think about, too much to consider whether it's Pitt and Tarantino Nessa is talking about, or whether she's smuggled Schubert into the hospital, so I just say, 'Great. Thanks,' and look at Scott, who's slipped the T-shirt on and is carefully folding the blanket up and lying it on the bed across Isa's feet.

The weight of it makes her stir and she peers at us sleepily. 'Mum?' she whispers.

'I'm not going far,' I tell her. 'I'm just going for a coffee with — '

' — my daddy. My hero. I love you, Daddy,' she finishes. She smiles, a little smugly, and closes her eyes again, and I

161

think she's heard more than we gave her credit for.

'God love her,' says the nurse with a huge smile. 'I can tell she's a daddy's girl, that one.'

And she bustles out of the room, leaving me staring behind her, wondering if Isa is being just a little sarcastic, or if she genuinely means what she just said.

# 14

## Scott

We're sitting outside of the hospital, two paper cups from the coffee shop on the ground by our feet as we perch, side by side, on a bench in the evening sunshine.

It's good to be breathing fresh air. I must confess that when the smoke was curling around us in the shop, I wondered for a moment whether I'd ever breathe fresh air again. But it just seemed more important to rescue Isa.

'It's nice to be in the fresh air,' Liza says.

I smile. 'I was just thinking about that. I can't get the smell of smoke out of my nose, though.'

Liza laughs, shakily. 'It's pretty acrid. Look. I don't know if I thanked you properly for rescuing Isa. It's pretty much a blur.'

I pretend to think for a minute. 'Yep. I do recall that you said 'thank you' a couple of times.'

She shakes her head and her hair flips around. 'I probably did. The truth of the matter is . . . ' Her voice fades out.

Clearly, she can't verbalise anything about the truth of the matter, so I take a deep breath and fill in the blanks for her. 'The truth of the matter is, I'm certain I've just discovered I have a daughter I knew nothing about. I really don't know what to do from here.'

She turns and looks right into my eyes. 'I don't know either.' She dips her head and stares at the ground, blushes a little bit and looks back at me. 'That is, if we're right and we did — you know — get together.'

'Okay — quick question.' I force a smile onto my face. 'What happened when you left the flat?'

She pauses for a second, then leans down and rolls her trousers up. There's

164

a scar on her leg — just a narrow one — but it's at about the height of a coffee table.

'I fell over a guitar. I think it broke, and then the glass coffee table attacked me. It *deferably* attacked me.'

My stomach flips and I take a deep breath. 'The guitar never really recovered,' I tell her. 'I felt bad that we smashed Davy's table. It took some explaining.'

'Hmm. Maybe not as much explaining as getting pregnant did,' she says wryly. 'I come from a small village near Glen Quaich, in Inverness-shire. I didn't stay there long afterwards. I don't particularly like being the subject of village gossip.'

I feel myself grow hot and look away. 'Yeah. Puts it into perspective, I guess.'

'Definitely.'

'I would have done something if I'd known — '

' — I had no way of finding you. I don't know what I would have asked you to do even if we had found each other again.' She looks down at her hands. 'For God's sake, we didn't even know each other's names, never mind exchange numbers.' She looks up again and fixes me with her eyes. 'I thought you were a music student. I hung around that part of the campus to see if I could see you. Until I got too fat and too obvious. I tried. I just don't know what I would have said if I'd seen you. 'Nice tattoo', maybe.'

I shake my head. 'You wouldn't have seen me. I wasn't even at that university. I was staying with my friend for the night. I moved on in the morning. In the opposite direction to Nessa and the rest of my weird family. Towards Glasgow.'

She laughs, as I hoped she would. 'Nessa is lovely. She's . . . unique.'

'Unique is one way of putting it. I think she's a bit of a witch, like our great-great granny was. She already seemed to know about . . . us.'

'Yes, she mentioned the witch thing to me once before.' She dips her head and colours, but she doesn't expand on the statement. Her hands are clasped on her lap now, and I don't know whether it would be appropriate to take one of them.

So I don't.

'I did try to follow you,' I add. It seems important that she knows this. 'I followed you downstairs. But you'd gone. You'd crossed the river — ' Her head comes up and I look at her sharply.

'That's what I do.' Her voice is little more than a whisper. 'I run. I follow water courses and I run with the current. Or I used to. Until I had Isa. When I found out I was pregnant, and I knew what my family's reaction was, I ran from the Glen. Just as far as I could. I followed the rivers as far as I could and ended up here. Somehow.'

## Liza

I'm a bit embarrassed that I called Scott a *sluagh*. I don't think I can ever

167

tell him that, no matter what happens in the future.

I don't really want to think about the father of my child as a malevolent, unforgiven 'Dead'. Nessa was pretty firm on the fallen angel thing anyway, as I recall. But there's that phrase again — 'the father of my child'.

I think I'm going to hyperventilate.

'You okay?' Scott asks. 'It's a lot to take in. It's been the day from hell.'

It's a bit too close to the mark for what I've just been thinking, so I stand up, a bit too quickly. Scott is on his feet next to me in an instant.

I turn to him and force a smile. 'Definitely. I need to move around. I've sat down for far too long.'

'Okay.' He nods. 'Do you want me to — you know — move around with you?' Then he blushes and I find that mildly comical, as I think he's remembering the last time we moved around together.

Then I think that it's not really very comical at all.

Then I start to cry.

Scott's arm snakes around me, a little bit awkwardly at first, but then it settles there like it was meant to rest across my shoulders in such a way. He pulls me a little closer but doesn't look at me. He's staring across the neat hospital gardens, and I imagine it's just as difficult for him. I've had eleven years or so to get used to Isa being around. He's had, what, eleven minutes?

Okay, so that's an exaggeration, but he hasn't had very long.

After a few more minutes, he clears his throat and frowns. 'Do you think Nessa smuggled Schubert into the hospital?' he asks.

Suddenly, I'm half-laughing through my tears and I nod. 'Yes. Yes, I do. I swear I saw his ear.'

'It twitched, didn't it? It twitched in the bag.'

'There was a definite twitch.'

Scott ducks down and smiles at me, right into my eyes, then he lifts his spare

169

hand and cups my chin, tilting my face upwards.

His eyes soften. 'I have to be honest. I'm not handling this well,' he tells me. 'I make jokes when it's inappropriate and I don't know what else to say.'

'Yes. Isa's never short of a comeback either,' I say, then I bite my lip. 'Sorry. I'm going to be trying to see you in her for months now.' I take a deep breath and move out of his embrace. 'I've looked for — you — her father, that is — in her all her life. She never ceases to amaze me. But as she's getting older, I see more of him — of *you* — in there. God knows what she'll be like as an adult.' My shoulders feel chilly where his arm was, and I can still feel the gentle pressure of his fingers on my chin. But it's time to say it. 'I understand if you want nothing to do with us. We've managed fine for all these years, and I don't want you to feel like you have to be part of her life.' *Her* life, I think to myself. Not *my* life. Not *our* lives. *Her* life. Heaven forbid he thinks he should be obliged to be part of anything. 'It was mere chance we met again,' I go on, 'and if I hadn't been out that night, I doubt we *would* have met again.' I wave my arm vaguely in the direction I think the shop is; or was, rather. There's a little sickening lurch in my stomach as I think of it. 'I doubt you'd be the sort of person who would wander into an arty-crafty-booky shop.'

'Maybe.' He shrugs. 'You might be right. But the fact is I did bump into you and we did meet again.' He falls silent and folds his arms. It's his defensive gesture, I know that now.

'I'm sorry.'

He shakes his head. 'No. It's nobody's fault. Just if I hadn't whipped my damn shirt off, then you would never have known. My bad.'

I begin to nod but catch a certain nuance in his tone. 'Hang on. *I* would never have known?'

'Yeah.'

'So *you* knew?'

He shrugs. 'Not for sure. But there was something. You were drunk in the bar. It was when you stumbled. I thought I'd seen you before, and then when I met Isa in the courtyard . . . she was too much like Nessa was at that age. Too much like myself. But then I thought there are a hundred million pre-teens with attitudes out there — why would this one be any different? I don't know when the pieces started to fit together in my head, but they did and that was the picture they made. Like a really bizarre jigsaw. I just thought I was being stupid.'

'Well I obviously made a lasting impression on you,' I say sarcastically.

'As I did on you,' he replies mildly. 'You didn't even have a clue that we *might* have met before the bar, did you?'

I lower my gaze. It's not exactly true. But I definitely knew his eyes were dangerous — eyes *like* his were dangerous. Exciting dangerous. But I'm not going to tell him that. It seems better to be vague.

'You were a little familiar in some ways,' I say stiffly. 'But it could just be that I've met a lot of opinionated men in my time, who act all nice and interested in you, then turn into pains in the backside when you meet them again.' My face burns, and I hope he can't tell that I'm blushing but that seems a crazy hope, to be honest.

There's a little snort and I think he must have laughed. 'You're a terrible liar.' His voice is soft. 'You've thought of that night and what we, crazily, felt for each other probably as much as I have over the years.'

'Perhaps. Anyway.' I stand up straight and shake my hands out, just to rid myself of some nervous energy. 'What do we do now? The ball is in your court, Scott. I've told you my thoughts. You can think about it. I'm going back to my daughter.' I turn on my heel and feel the flames rush through my cheeks again. She'll never

just be 'my' daughter again, will she?
Not now I've met Scott again.
Not now I've met her father again.

# 15

## Scott

I pause for just a second and then hurry after Liza. No matter what our history is, Isa is my daughter as well, and I need to make sure she's okay. I need to see her.

Isa looks a lot brighter now. She's woken up properly, and she's lounging against the pillows looking positively regal, her red hair brushed out and tied into two bunches with bright green ribbons; Nessa's doing, I suspect.

There's a suspicious looking fat bulge in the bed, under the covers, next to Isa and I stare at it. The bulge moves a bit and I can see Isa's hand resting on it under the sheets. It looks like she's stroking it. I have a feeling I know what the bulge is, as there are one or two black hairs on the white sheets and

Nessa and Isa both look far too innocent. Ewan just looks pained.

'Animals are excellent therapy,' says Nessa. I just shake my head and Liza stares in horror.

'Is it — ' begins Liza, but she can't continue, as a doctor comes in.

'Time for us to leave then,' says Nessa. She looks at Isa, wide-eyed. 'Will I take Mr Snuggles with me?'

Mr Snuggles? Mr bloody *Snuggles*?

Nessa looks at the doctor. 'I brought my niece's favourite stuffed animal in to bring her a bit of comfort. I'll just take him home, and he can keep her bed warm for her coming back.'

'Oh I'll not be a minute.' The doctor smiles and looks affectionately at the big, fat, bulge in the bed.

'It's not a problem,' says Nessa with a saccharin-sweet smile.

Then she peels the covers back and Schubert is lying there, eyes closed, motionless, barely even breathing, his legs stuck out at the sides.

He looks like a bad taxidermy advert,

never mind Mr bloody Snuggles.

Nessa sort of half scoops him, half pours him into her bag, and he puddles in the bottom of it, every inch a stuffed toy, not moving at all.

Then she closes the bag up and hoists it over her shoulder and turns to me. 'We'll see you later, Scotty. You did a very brave thing today.' She stands on tiptoe and kisses me, which is the most affectionate my sister has been for a long time.

I hug her back, and I mean it. 'Thanks, Nessa.'

She pats me on the arm and turns to Ewan. 'Come on. Let's get Mr Snuggles back for Isa,' she says and leads the way out of the room.

'See you later,' says Ewan, looking a curious mix of apologetic, impressed and perplexed, as he follows Nessa out.

'See you,' I say.

'See you,' adds the doctor. He does his bits and bobs, writes things down and nods cheerfully, before he also leaves muttering reassuring comments.

He has a few positive words with a shocked-looking Liza, who nods mutely, thanks him, then stares out of the door where Nessa and Schubert and Ewan disappeared. 'That was — ' she starts, then shakes her head. 'How? She's . . .'

'Brazen?' I offer. 'And Ewan's quite mad to stay with her?'

'I don't know. But they're happy aren't they? They're really *happy*.'

Just then, Isa's voice interrupts us. 'Mummy, I don't want a rabbit anymore. I want a cat. Daddy — can you get me a cat? Please? A kitten or something?' She gazes at the door wistfully. 'A big, fat, snuggly cat. Please?'

I look at her and my mouth moves, but no words come out. I see Liza out of the corner of my eye. She folds her arms and a little smile starts to lift the corner of her lips. It's tiny, but there's definitely one there.

It's like she's waiting for me to fall down the parental rabbit-hole.

I take the coward's way out. I hear myself parroting what every parent must have said to their child at one time or another.

'We'll see,' I tell her weakly. 'We'll see.'

## Liza

In the end, they kept Isa in overnight, and she came home the next day. But it doesn't make it any easier for me to deal with Scott and the new-found knowledge that we've created a life between us. If anything, it's more awkward because I feel we've done nothing but dance around each other in my tiny terraced flat every time he's come to visit.

And waves of flame and embarrassment keep flooding into my very soul every time I think of him and all those feelings I had when we met and spent that one, perfect night together.

Because it *was* perfect. I can admit

that to myself now. And the reason I ran was because I *knew* it was perfect, and I didn't want to be tied down. I was a free spirit and wanted to stay that way, because the whole idea of commitment terrified me and I knew this guy was 'The One', even if he didn't. It was the only thing I could do — run, and follow the water course to safety.

And look how that bloody turned out. Fate is one weird concept. Because didn't I get Isabel out of it? And look how we met again, and how Isa forged that bond unbreakably. Things are never going to be the same again, and I don't know how that makes me feel. I kind of want to run again. But then I don't.

My brain is boggled.

And now, it's the end of the week, and Isa isn't particularly bothered about seeing either of us. She's disappeared into her bedroom, leaving us mutely acknowledging each other's company and now it is *so* damned awkward I have a sweat on, and you can tell Scott is itching to get away.

'Tell me if I'm bothering you by being here,' he keeps saying. 'Just tell me to go and I'll go.'

'You're not bothering me,' I keep saying, because in an odd way he isn't. It is, on some levels, kind of nice to make two cups of tea, ask if he wants a sandwich at lunchtime, ask if he doesn't mind staying with Isa whilst I nip out to the shop for some milk or bread.

But then in other ways, it's just plain weird.

Scott sort of fills my lounge and he fills my kitchen and he definitely fills my yard. This afternoon, for instance, I've come back and he's made a start weeding between the old, broken paving slabs and tidying things up.

I push the door open and clear my throat a bit. 'I'm back. With the milk.' I hold up the carton, hoping there aren't tell-tale sweaty circles under my arm-pits, because of having the aforementioned sweat on in his presence.

But he stands up and grins, half-guiltily. 'Sorry. It looked like it needed doing. I'm a designer. I like to make sense out of chaos.' He stands there, peering around the yard through his thick, dark fringe. 'I think you could do a lot out here. You could fit everything in if you wanted.'

'It's tiny. No way,' I scoff, forgetting my sweaty armpits. It's quite cool out here and I venture outside to stand next to him. 'Isa will never get her swing out here.' He knows, of course, how much she wants a swing at home as well as the one she used in the courtyard at Phoenix Antiques — or rather where Phoenix Antiques had been. I still haven't gone to see it. 'Yes, of course she could have a swing.' Scott pulls out a notebook and a pen from his pocket, and I'm surprised. I never expected him to carry that sort of stuff around.

'Look,' he continues. He makes a few marks on the page. At the back of the yard, maybe using a quarter of the space up, he demonstrates where a raised lawn could go, with two steps up to it where a swing set/climbing frame combo could go. Beside that, is a sitting area beneath a gazebo, where he's drawn a table and chairs. In front of the play-lawn, he's sketched in a little waterfall, running down into a tiny pond. He's put in raised flower beds and rockeries along the two long walls, but still it isn't finished. I watch in fascination as my dream garden takes shape on the paper.

'You could pave it all properly, or gravel it, see, then you wouldn't need to weed it. And you could have a couple of pots — just there, perhaps — and decorate your gazebo with honeysuckle or climbing roses and fairy lights.' He looks up again, narrowing his eyes, his pen poised over the paper. 'Yeah. It would work. Bay trees. Or topiary.' He nods and puts a swirly, flourishy tree by the steps up to the play-lawn then turns and grins at me. 'So much you can do, if you put your mind to it.' He rips the page out

183

of the notebook and hands it to me.

'Wow. Thanks. I'd love it to look like that.' I smile down at the sketch. 'Although Isa now swears that her life won't be complete without a sunken trampoline.'

'Bloody dangerous,' grumbles Scott. He shoves his hands in his pockets and glowers at the yard. 'Too many broken limbs from those things.'

'Her argument is if it's sunken, she can't fall off it.'

'She can fall down the side.'

'I don't think that's quite as likely.'

'Whatever.' He turns to me and nods to the sketch. 'I don't want to outstay my welcome, that is if there is even a welcome here, but if ever you want anything doing for your yard there, just give me a shout, okay?'

'Thanks.' I fold the picture up and put it in my pocket. 'It's unlikely I could ever afford it, but you never know. And it's only rented, so I don't really know what I'm even at liberty to do.'

'No, I suppose not. Oh well. You never know. Okay. Goodbye, Liza.' He nods briskly and turns on his heel, his buckles clinking against his boots.

As he walks off, I put my hand in my pocket again and feel the folded-up square in there; then, somehow, I feel a horrible sense of loss.

I think that I wish we could have had more than just discussions in the yard. I think I wish that we could start again.

I think I wish that we could become proper friends.

Proper friends would be a start, I reason. It would be a good start.

But I don't know if I'd ever be sure we were friends because we liked each other, or friends because we had to be, because of Isa.

I hear myself shouting after him. 'Scott. I'm sorry.'

He pauses and turns. He looks perplexed, as he might do, because I can't remember being too horrible to him recently, now I come to think about it.

'What about?' he asks, frowning.

'About calling you a *sluagh sidhe*.'

'*What?*' he repeats, taking a couple of steps towards me again.

'A *sluagh sidhe*,' I say, my cheeks burning. I begin to wish I really did have a small pond, because I could stick my head in it right now and end it all before I have to explain anything else to him. But I can't seem to stop myself — there's just no filter. 'It's a — '

'I *know* what a *sluagh sidhe* is.' He walks right back up to me, and he's right in front of me and his eyes are burning into mine and I'm absolutely mesmerised. 'It's a long time since I've been called a fallen angel, my little *cuachag*,' he murmurs, and a smile plays about his lips. I feel my cheeks flame again — there is something ridiculously and dangerously seductive in those eyes and those lips, and I think I'm falling somewhere I don't think I can climb back out of.

'*Cuachag*,' I murmur, not taking my eyes off him. 'Like a dangerous water sprite? Just because I've got curly hair and I'm from Glen Quaich?' Little does he know.

'*Cuachag*,' he confirms.

Okay, so he knows.

'I'm not always . . . *as* . . . dark as a *cuachag*. Not really.'

'Really?' He doesn't seem convinced. And why should he be?

Then it seems like I blink, and he's gone.

# 16

## Scott

A *sluagh sidhe*?

I must confess, I find it a bit amusing. If you asked Nessa about Liza, she'd just sniff and say she was very perceptive. Our family history is a bit mixed up, I'll agree. God alone knows what we all are.

But I do like the idea of the fallen angel bit, rather than the malevolent and unforgiving creature that folklore suggests. I do try to channel the 'angel' thing a bit more, but it's not always easy. It's part of the reason I got my tattoo — as a kind of reminder not to let that dark side and all its associated demons rule my way of thinking. It's too easy to forget that, and be ruthless and cruel; especially when a person is trying to set their own business up and make a success of it.

It's too easy to trample over people on the way there, and I do cringe a bit when I think of how I tried to snaffle Phoenix Antiques from under Liza's nose. Well, she was a force to be reckoned with in the end.

I shake my head and grin as I clamber onto my motorbike. A *sluagh sidhe* indeed.

And she *is* a *cuachag* — no doubt about it.

Then I'm serious for a moment. With our genes, and a witch in the family, and Celtic folklore dictating one of my brother's lives, and God-knows-what dictating the others, what the hell will Isa turn out like? It seems a thing to wonder on, as a famous poet once said. And I know that I want to be around to see it; to see Isa grow up and to try to make up for the time we've lost.

To buy her a bloody kitten if she wants one. To buy her a hundred bloody kittens. And to buy her a guitar and a grand piano and a part in a West

End show, if I can do it.

The thought sobers me up instantly, and I stop smiling and frown instead as I switch the bike on.

Our daughter's genes are indeed an incredible cocktail.

## Liza

This morning, Monday, Isa eventually declared she was bored and demanded that she go back to school. I've tried to put that odd conversation with Scott out of my head, and I think I feel a bit stronger and more able to face Phoenix Antiques. Or what's left of it, anyway.

By the time I get there, Scott is already in amongst the burnt-out wreckage of the building, apparently poking around and salvaging what he can — which isn't a lot. The piano is just a big hulk of charred wood, and I see him draw his hand wistfully over the blackened surface. I remember, a little painfully, watching him and Isa thrash

190

out 'Dance of the Sugar Plum Fairy'.

'Gives a whole new perspective on smashing guitars up after a rock concert, doesn't it?' I say, standing in the doorway, feeling a little awkward. I hope he might have forgiven me or, even better, forgotten about me calling him names yesterday.

Scott turns and half-smiles. 'Yeah. That's sacrilege. I'd never destroy my guitar.'

'Too expensive?' I ask, stepping over the threshold and into the still-damp, smelly shell of the building, feeling a bit bolder.

'Too many memories,' he replies, without looking at me, and so it's impossible to read his eyes and see what that infers. I wonder if he's thinking about our highly potent one-night stand, and there's a tiny corner of my mind that raises its head curiously when I think about that.

But it's pointless to dwell on it. Scott's memories are probably nothing of the sort.

Instead, he finally turns to me and frowns. 'Electrical fault. That's what they're saying. God knows what caused it.' He shrugs and steps over some charred ash that I think was a pile of books or perhaps some cushions that said 'Live, Laugh, Love'. I feel my mouth turn down and begin to wobble as I stare at the mess.

'Hey, hey, hey,' says Scott. He's next to me in an instant, pulling me towards him, enfolding me in his arms — and I'm happy to stay there, I really am. Because if my face is crushed against his soft grey T-shirt and I squeeze my eyes shut and all I can smell is his woodsmoke and spice aftershave and his fabric conditioner, then I can pretend I'm not standing in the burnt-out wreckage of my dreams.

It seems there's no bloody escape from the grotty, hairless baby rodents at the vet's. This was my last chance. My last bloody chance.

'Come on now.' He stands away from me a little and puts his fingers beneath my chin, tilting my face up towards his. 'At least the little one's safe. We got her out. All this is insured. It's all replaceable. And perhaps it's best the pashminas went the distance.'

'I know, I know.' And I do know. It's just seeing it all like this and thinking about what might have happened if Scott hadn't come at that moment. What if we hadn't realised Isa was in there? 'Oh God, oh God,' I moan. Then it all comes to the surface, and there's nothing I can do to stop it.

And Scott just stands there, holding me, rocking me, murmuring things to me that I don't even comprehend. Then I look up at him and open my mouth to say something and there's a strange look in those green eyes, and he bends down to me and we're kissing and we're holding each other and we're both lost.

Lost. Absolutely lost.

And I don't think there's anything I can do about it.

And I don't think there's anything I

*want* to do about it, either, which, weirdly, is a whole new thing to cry over.

# 17

## Scott

It's instinctive. I can't help it, I can't help leaning into *that* kiss because it's so exactly where I need to be right now and no matter what our history, and the fact that we've largely locked horns over the last few months, I don't want to see her cry; and especially not in the shell of what was once her dream.

I want to make it all right for her. She's safe in my arms for now, and her hair is pulled back in a ponytail, and she isn't wearing a scrap of make-up and she looks so young and vulnerable. It's hard to think she's a mother and someone who danced on tables at university. It's hard to think that she's raised a child and kept strong all these years, only to be dragged down by this.

If I could change things, if I could go

back and not demand the top floor of Phoenix Antiques. If I hadn't met her that night in the bar when she told me about the empty building. If I had never started to teach Isa piano . . .

But I can't go there. Because then I might not have met Isa until she was grown up — if at all — and I might not just have missed ten years of her life, but missed twice that.

And I might have been too late to pick things up with Liza. Because despite all that, and despite the fact that we *do* have this history, I think I've fallen for her and fallen hard. If Isa didn't exist, I realise with a stab of clarity, I'd still feel the same about Liza.

I think I knew that from the moment I saw her, eleven years ago.

I lean forward and bury my face in the top of her hair. 'I'm sorry,' I say. 'I'm so sorry.' But I'm not quite sure what I'm sorry about. I can't be sorry about making Isa. I just can't be. Maybe I'm sorry that it's taken so long to find out.

Maybe I'm sorry about the building burning down — and I am — but buildings and contents are replaceable. Ten years of my daughter's life — eleven years with Liza — aren't.

She brings her arms around me and her shoulders stop shaking, and I wait a moment to make sure she's calmed down before pulling away gently. There are damp patches on my T-shirt from her tears and the cool air chills my skin through the thin cotton.

'Let's go,' I tell her. 'There's nothing much we can do here. Let's go.'

'All the stock — '

' — Doesn't matter.'

'Your piano.'

'It was never my piano. It doesn't matter.'

'Your design — thing — outlet, consultancy, whatever upstairs.'

'Just an experiment.'

'My job at the vet's! I'll need to pick up my hours again!'

'They'll take you back. And if they don't, we'll worry about it then.'

'Isa — '

' — Isa's fine. Come on. Let's go.'

'Where?' Her voice catches on a sob as she looks at the devastation around us. 'Where the hell can we go from here.'

My lips curl into a smile and I drop a kiss on her mouth. I suspect it's not the answer she was after.

'From where?' I ask. 'From Methven Street? We can go anywhere you like.'

She just stares at me dumbly, as if she realises what she's said.

'Or,' I say carefully, 'we can see where *we* go from here. And my house might be the best option just at the minute. I have a kettle and tea bags and coffee. What more do you want?'

'I don't know. But I know I'd like to go to your house. If that's okay.'

'It's fine. D'you mind hopping on the back of my bike? I've got a spare helmet in the storage box.'

She looks up at me and there's the hint of a wobbly smile there. 'Do I have to hang on tightly?' she asks.

198

'Very tightly,' I say.

And strangely, we laugh and our foreheads meet and our arms wrap around each other again, and I know it's going to be a long bike ride back to my house.

## Liza

Of course, we don't have coffee or tea or anything of the sort.

We roar through the streets of Edinburgh, probably exceeding the speed limit, and my eyes almost cross as I see the kerbs whizz past us looking like clay spinning on a potter's wheel. We head away from the centre, away from the Royal Mile, away from the New Town. We drive along a narrow street lined with big, old-fashioned detached houses, and we take a sudden turn into the gates of one of them. I cling on as we head up the drive and the bike comes to a standstill, next to a van emblazoned with the words *Scott*

*McCreadie Interior Design.*

Scott is off the bike in an instant. He more or less lifts me from the back seat as I pull the helmet off my head, and we hurry towards the front door. I'm vaguely aware of a huge, airy hallway and a wide, sweeping staircase before he takes my hand again and we pound up the stairs, two at a time.

I realise there's a curious sound as we run, and it's me giggling like I'm reckless and wild and carefree again, and Scott laughing with me, a deep chuckling sound that's delicious to hear. He stops half-way up where the staircase goes back on itself and wraps his arms around me and we kiss and we laugh and then we run up the next flight.

We hurtle along the landing and he throws a door open and I see a huge, king-size bed in front of me.

I hesitate just for a second and he stops and turns to me. 'Is it okay? Is this what you want? Tell me to stop and I will.'

He looks so concerned and his half-fringe is sort of sticking up and his eyebrows are knitted, and I shake my head and laugh again. 'I want it. I do. I'm just out of practise. I'm sorry.'

Scott laughs too and pulls me close. I think he's going to say something corny like 'I'm not', but he doesn't.

'We'll take it slowly,' he says instead. 'If you want to stop, we'll stop. If you want to go easy, we'll go easy.'

'And what if I don't want to do any of those things?' I tease, loosening my hand from his and reaching for his grey T-shirt. 'What if I just want to go for it? I'm still *me*. I'm still crazy about green-eyed, opinionated bad boys. I'm still kind of crazy . . . about you.'

'Then we'll go for it!' he replies, his eyes twinkling into mine as he reaches for the button on my jeans. The faint brush of his fingers on my bare stomach is enough to send me into overdrive and fireworks start shooting around my system as my breath catches and I tilt my head back, my eyes closed, my lips half-open.

He leans down and kisses me gently, all over my neck and I seriously think I'm going to explode.

I tilt my head to the side, and he follows the line of my neck and I cling to him, and we kiss and we get in a muddle and there are clothes everywhere.

And it's wonderful.

I don't regret it for a minute.

I don't regret anything.

And when I catch sight of his angel wings again, I run my fingers down his spine and he shivers. Then he turns to me and eleven years just slip away.

# 18

## Scott

I remembered that first night, which is a bizarre thing to say. But I seemed to know exactly, instinctively, what to do to make her squirm and giggle and, finally, go into orbit.

I'm not claiming any special powers, because she knew exactly how to do the same things for me — well, maybe not the giggling thing, but you understand what I mean.

'So, what was all that about then?' I ask her afterwards, nuzzling into her hair, rubbing my cheeks against her gorgeous, copper curls.

'God knows,' she says. 'The fact we came so close to losing everything that matters?' There's a pause and I know she's talking about Isa. I pull her closer and she snuggles in to me. It feels deliciously decadent to be in bed in the middle of the day.

'But we didn't. So, is this a celebration of life? A way of us saying 'to hell with everything else'? A 'let's stop pretending we hate each other', kind of thing?'

I can feel her smile against my shoulder. 'Maybe.' She head-butts me gently. 'I still hate you. I think I could easily hate you.'

'But deep down you love opinionated bad boys.'

'No.' She shakes her head and my skin pulls taut beneath her cheeks. 'Deep down I love *green-eyed*, opinionated bad boys. I just don't always show it.'

'You showed me just before. Two or three times, I think.'

She laughs and curls in closer to me.

Just then, there's a ring at the doorbell and she stiffens. I swear and stay rigidly still. Perhaps they'll go away if I don't engage.

There's another ring, then a rattle at

the door and I frown. 'I'm not going down,' I state. 'I'm not expecting anyone.'

'Maybe you should,' says Liza. She uncurls and sits up in bed, her knees draw up, her arms around them, her hair, loosened from its ponytail, spilling down over her shoulders. I feel a stirring again and smile lazily at her, raising my eyebrows in an unspoken question.

Liza laughs and pulls her knees up closer. 'No. Go and answer the door. It might be the police.'

The thought instantly sobers us up, and I slide out of bed, grabbing my T-shirt and some jogging bottoms.

'Nice tattoo,' she calls after me as I head out of the door, and I duck my head and grin as I hurry down the stairs.

I jump down the last couple and pitch up at the front door. I pull it open and there's nobody there, but there is a box on the step, tied up with a green ribbon. I frown and bend down to pick it up. It's heavy and weighty, and I jiggle it around experimentally. Something subtly slides around inside, and I bring it into the hallway and shut the door, tugging at the ribbon to open the box.

The ribbon slips open, and the memory of green ribbon around Isa's bunches at the hospital makes a cog begin to whir. Nessa.

The box is, I see, a picnic hamper. From Valvona & Crolla, no less: a high-end Italian delicatessen with the most mouth-watering cakes, chocolates and wines I can think of. Inside the hamper, is — not unexpectedly — a bottle of champagne, some chocolate truffles and, surprise, surprise, a cake which smells deliciously of candied fruits and raisins. A gift tag has fallen onto the floor, and I realise it was attached to the ribbon. I pick it up and turn it over: it's a picture of Schubert. A bloody big photograph of his face, with him looking eminently fat and superior, as only he can.

My mouth twitches and before another second has passed I'm laughing and shaking my head and running back upstairs to find Liza, who has lain down again and she's staring dreamily at the ceiling with her hands behind her head.

'We have a gift,' I tell her. 'Seems like my sister was one step ahead of us, as usual.' I sit on the bed and spread the goodies out before us as she sits up. 'When do we need to collect Isa from school?'

'Three o'clock,' Liza says, picking up the truffles and reading the box.

'So, there's nothing stopping you having a glass of this, if I go and collect her?' I ask. 'I'll bring her back here and we can get a pizza in or something. She'll like that, won't she?'

Liza tears her gaze away from the truffles and puts the box down. She stares at me, wide-eyed. 'I don't know . . . ' she begins. 'Maybe she'll be awkward with you. Maybe she'll just want me there. It's her first day back, after all.'

But I take her hands in mine and bring them to my lips, and kiss them. 'I insist,' I tell her. 'Really I do. And I'll save my glass for later.'

There's a beat while she considers it, and I can see the conflicting emotions in her eyes. Then she seems to make a decision. 'I'll save mine too,' she says. 'And we can have one together. With our pizza.'

'Excellent.'

'And we'll get a taxi back to the flat afterwards.'

'You can stay here if you want.'

'Not tonight. Let Isa get used to things first. Just not tonight.'

I still have her hands in mine, and I kiss them again and run my thumbs gently over her knuckles. 'Let her get used to things.' It's a nice phrase. It's a good phrase. And I know without a shadow of a doubt that 'things' are going to be wonderful; they're going to be very wonderful after all.

But Liza seems unsure again. 'Her school's a couple of miles away from here — ' Liza begins, as if she suddenly feels that there should at least be *some* protestation, but I cut her off. You just know when things have fallen into place — call it a sixth sense, call it something to do with my genetic history, call it what you will. But I *know*. And she knows as well. She absolutely does.

I grin. 'That's fine. I have a motorbike. And a spare helmet.'

Liza looks at me for a moment, sizing me up, wondering whether I'm safe enough on the motorbike to transport her child. Our child.

'You'll drive slowly,' she states.

'I'll drive slowly,' I confirm.

'Okay,' she says. 'Three o'clock. But you can't be late for her. That's unforgiveable.' Her eyes drift past me to the clock. Her fingers travel up my arm and onto my shoulder. Her hand grips it and she begins to pull me towards her, a light in her eye that spells a little bit of danger and a lot of fun. 'Having said that, we still have a fair bit of time.'

'I should chill the champagne first,' I

say, even as I feel myself responding to her touch.

'No, you shouldn't,' she says.

'Fair enough,' I say.

And I don't.

* * *

A little bit later on, and I'm thinking that this could go either way.

I'm sitting outside the school on my motorbike, drumming my fingers on the handlebars and whistling. Somewhere inside the low stone building, a bell rings. The doors open and, within moments, children are spilling out into the yard and onto the pavement and running towards various adults.

God, it's like some horrific sort of world I never even knew existed. I sit up straighter, though. I suppose it's something I'm going to have to get used to.

Isa tumbles out with the rest, arguing with a blonde-haired girl with French plaits down either side of her head:

Sophie, I guess. Isa hovers in the yard, drawing to a halt, her eyes going to where her mother must usually collect her when she's not at work dealing with hairless rodents.

Seeing the space empty, she looks around, a momentary expression of panic flitting across her creamy-white, freckled face. Her eyes eventually settle on me, waiting just outside the gates on my motorbike. I've taken my helmet off and tucked it under my arm so she can be sure it's me, but even so I raise my hand and wave at her.

There's a beat, then her face breaks into a huge grin and she comes running over to me. Sophie hesitates and then follows her. Then I see a trail of mummies and children all looking in our direction as Isa waves wildly at me.

'Look!' she shrieks as she runs towards me, beaming. 'Look Sophie. It's my daddy. He's the one that pulled me out of the fire. Look!' The grumpy, attitude-ridden pre-teen is gone, and a little girl, my little girl, is running towards me. I'm not stupid; I know, coming from a family with a total of five siblings, that children can be difficult. There will be days to come where she'll think she hates me. She'll think she hates Liza. And she'll tell us that too. There are days where it'll hurt to even look at her, and days where we'll all want our own space. Maybe I'm a bit of a novelty at the minute — maybe she's always wanted a dad, whatever sort of dad it is. But I'm going to be the best dad I can be. I owe her that much.

'Cool bike!' Sophie yells, drawing to a halt a few feet away. She gives Isa a thumbs-up before she runs off to her own mum; a lady who is staring very curiously in our direction. I can't help but grin and wave at the mum who is, I suspect, a friend of Liza's.

And I know I'll never stop loving Liza or Isabel. With my genetics, some things are pretty much written in the stars — and that's one of them.

But for now, at least, I exhale, letting

out a breath I didn't know I was holding in, and then I laugh. I wave back at Isa and climb off the bike. Instinctively, I open my arms and Isa runs straight into them, jumping at me, her feet lifting off the ground, the weight of her bag swinging dangerously to one side so she almost unbalances me.

'Hello little one,' I say.

'Hello!' she says. Her eyes move to the bike, and I lower her back onto the ground. 'Am I getting a lift home?' Her eyes, so like mine, shine with avarice and I laugh again.

'Not quite. We're going to my house. I think you'll like it there. Your mum's there as well. We're going to get a pizza for tea. Is that okay?'

She nods and I hand her the helmet. She plonks it on her head and as she stares at me through the visor, her red hair hidden, I get that little shock again where I feel that I'm almost looking in a mirror. I fasten the chin-strap for her and help her on the bike.

'Hold tight,' I say. 'Don't let go.'

'I won't. Oh. Do you have a piano at your house?'

I smile into my own visor as I kick-start the bike. 'Wait and see,' I tell her. 'Wait and see.'

## Liza

We're having some drinks after our pizza and there's still a faint smell of garlic wafting around the kitchen. It was all very delicious, I have to say, and the champagne is going down a treat.

Scott's talking about the strange, square room at the top of his house. He calls it 'The Turret Room'.

'It was originally going to be my study,' he says, 'but then I realised I wouldn't get much work done in there, because I just wanted to stare out of the windows. So I had one of the old stable blocks converted into a workshop. That's where I do a lot of my business.'

'But I thought your business was in

Glasgow?' I tear a slice off the leftover garlic bread and lick my fingers as the butter and the herbs drip deliciously down them.

'It is. That's my main shop. I relocated and decided I needed a visible presence here in Edinburgh. I kept my flat on at Glasgow, and stayed with my parents here — torture — for a while until I got a couple of rooms in this place habitable, then moved in and continued the work around myself.'

'So you came in from the west then.' My words are a statement of fact, not a question. It figures that he would come in from the west — my grannies' horrified faces flit into my mind for a moment, but I refuse to dwell on them. Neither one of them had time for me when I had Isa. Why would I give them time now?

'Aye.' His voice is amused. 'You could say that. That fact's not too much of a surprise then, I take it.'

'Not much.' I look around the

kitchen and see how much thought he's put into the place — from the skylights, to the wide benches, to the tiled breakfast bar where we are currently troughing our way through food, and the big windows that look out onto his vast expanse of landscaped garden.

'It's beautiful. If I ever need to recommend an interior designer, I'll recommend you.'

'Thanks. I did a grand job of Nessa's place too. You should see her kitchen. I should take you to her house again under better circumstances.'

I laugh. 'It's a date. So, the Turret Room became the music room here, then?'

'It did indeed.' Scott looks at Isa who's picking up bits of crispy cheese from the side of her plate and devouring them. It's good to see she's got her appetite back and her cough has almost gone now as well. You can barely see the mark on her forehead either which is even better.

Isa takes a huge glug of cola and

grins at us through the grease. 'I've always wanted a music room,' she announces.

'Well, there's a piano in there and a couple of guitars and some amps, as you've already seen.' Isa had belted up the stairs almost as soon as she'd come in to have a look at this musical Nirvana Scott had told her about. He shrugs and blushes a bit. 'I must have known. They're there for you, any time you want them. And if you recall, the piano is wooden coloured. Your mum won't ever be allowed to try and decorate that one.'

'Can I go up again after tea?'

'Sure,' says Scott. 'Like I said, any time you want.'

Isa wastes no time. 'Cool. See ya.' I notice she's pocketing two-thirds of the chocolate truffles which I had arranged prettily on a plate for pudding, as she's simultaneously sliding off the seat.

I hear her thunder upstairs and it's only a few moments until she is bashing out a tune on the piano.

I say bashing it out; she's actually pretty good. It's something from *Les Misérables*. She's clearly found a few bits of sheet music up there and it seems as if she's decided to work through them, as the tune suddenly changes into 'Bohemian Rhapsody', and I laugh.

'You've taught her well,' I tell him and he nods. No need, now, for him to deny it or brush it off.

'Are you finished?' He nods to my empty plate. 'I'll sort it out later — shall we take the drinks into the lounge?'

I agree. 'Why not.' Even though I realise we've almost finished the champagne, it'll be nice to just sit and curl up together. 'It's been a lovely day. Thank you. I'm sorry I had the meltdown this morning.' I blush thinking about the mess of what used to be Phoenix Antiques, and my stomach churns unpleasantly as I realise how much there still is to do.

'One thing at a time. Hey, when you've finished that glass, do you want

218

to see the garden? Or maybe open another bottle?'

I'm about to agree when I look at the clock and see that it's already seven o'clock. 'Damn. I'd love to do both of those things, but I should really call a taxi. Isa needs to have a bath and get settled. She should be exhausted from being back at school, but I suspect she'll be high as a kite from having had pizza and cola and free reign in the music room.'

Scott nods. 'Aye. Well. One day, hopefully, you won't have to get a taxi home. This house is way too big for me. It's a family house. How long have you got left on your lease at the flat?'

My stomach churns again and I take a deep breath. 'Three months.'

'Okay.' He nods. 'By then you might know if you can stand having me around a bit more permanently.'

'Scott!' I'm not sure if he's asking me to move in or what, but tonight, after all that food and all that champagne, the thought is eminently appealing.

He just grins at me and stands up. 'I'll call your taxi.' His smile, his *genuine* smile, I see with sudden realisation, is a carbon copy of Isa's. My heart lurches again as I think how similar they'd looked that first day on the piano. Why the hell had I not realised sooner?

'Okay. Thanks.' I feel a bit shaky again as I process that information. Then I watch him stand up and walk over to the phone, and my eyes drift over to the French doors that lead out into the garden.

I don't really want to get a taxi.

I want to stay here.

But I know that's out of the question tonight.

# 19

## Two Months Later

### Scott

'Mr Hogarth has an extensive portfolio of properties,' Nessa tells me snootily. 'I don't think you are in any position to doubt him.'

'Are you *sure* he's just a private detective?' I ask her, fixing her green stare exactly with my own green stare.

'Yes.' The comment does not invite further discussion, and I'm ashamed to say my gaze flickers away before hers does. She's sitting behind her desk at work, and she shuffles some papers importantly. 'Now, I'm rather busy, so please leave quietly.' She nods at the sign — *Mr Hogarth is out. Sorry.*

I lean forward, planting both my

palms on her desk and she stares meaningfully at them: 'Personal space is very important.' She raises her eyes and glares at me again.

'I agree,' I tell her coldly. 'And so is having space to do whatever the hell you want to do with it. Like having space for an arty-farty-crafty-dafty sort of shop. Our insurance money has come through for Phoenix Antiques. I want to help Liza set up again.'

'And space for your interior designer type outlet thing? Will that need to be taken into consideration?'

Now the challenge is all in her eyes.

I find myself lowering my gaze again. 'No.' I sigh. 'No. It's all going to be hers. I've got my stables. Well, my one stable. I have plans for the other one. My outlet can wait. I have my van. I can be mobile.' I push myself off the desk and fold my arms, studying my sister. 'Would any of that make a difference to what Mr Hogarth could offer me?'

Nessa just shrugs and clicks on her

mouse. 'Ah. I see. How utterly fortuitous,' she says. 'There's some information here about a property that has just come up for rental. Interesting.'

She leans forward and appears to be reading the screen, extremely slowly and extremely thoroughly. I suck my lips in and bite them hard, to prevent me from making any comments and to let her enjoy her moment.

'Hmmm.' Nessa tears her gaze away from the screen and looks at me again. 'Thank you for letting me read that very important email, Scotty.' She doesn't take her eyes off me, but I see her click a couple of times on her mouse and the printer behind her whirrs into action.

I want to throttle her, I really do. I remember why I had often hated her as a child.

She swings, very slowly, around in her seat and plucks the paper off the machine.

She then reads it again, equally

slowly and equally thoroughly, until I explode at her. 'For God's sake, Nessa! Just let me see it!' My sister looks up at me in some surprise, but she has pushed me far enough now. 'Nessa, please. Just let me see the damn thing.'

'There's no need to be so brusque, Scott.' She flings the paper at me scornfully. 'It seems as if you expect some sort of nepotism from me.'

'If you treat all your customers like you've just treated me, then I'm surprised you have repeat clientele,' I rage. 'It's the very opposite of nepotism that I've just experienced.'

'One can't get too complacent when one has friends and relations in high places,' replies Nessa, sniffing and folding her arms. 'Yet I do think you'll find that place very much to your taste.'

'Mow wow,' comes a muffled noise from beneath the desk. I duck down but can't see anything except the deep, bottom desk-drawer half-pulled out towards Nessa. She pushes it back in smartly and I stand up, baffled. 'Is that — ?'

Nessa blinks at me, blankly. 'I don't know what you mean. We've arranged a viewing for you this morning. In about half an hour. You'll find the key just in front of you there. I won't bother accompanying you.'

She nods to the desk which I had been leaning on moments before, and, sure enough, there is a key on it. I am thoroughly confused by this point and just look at her gormlessly.

'You're welcome.' She inclines her head politely.

I turn, clutching the print-out and the key as if I am in a trance, and walk out of the office.

There is a faint sound, as if a desk drawer has been pulled out again. 'Mow wow,' something says behind me, in an equally polite manner.

I just raise my hand and continue on my way and don't even turn to look back.

225

'I don't *care!*' rages Isa, thumping around and slamming doors. I shudder. The flat is far too small to have this mini — whirlwind stomping around.

She stomps out of the back door, stomps around the yard, kicks a few pebbles and strops back in. 'It's not *fair*. I don't see *why* I have to be a bloody *munchkin!*'

I suck my cheeks in and try not to react to the sweariness. 'Munchkins are highly important in *The Wizard of Oz* — '

' — *No!* Just *no!*'

'Isa — '

'NO!'

There is absolutely no reasoning with her when she's like this.

'I want to be Dorothy. And if I can't be Dorothy, I want to be the good witch. And if I can't be her, I'll be . . . I'll be . . . Toto. Yes. I'll be bloody Toto. Woof! Woof!' She drops onto all fours and starts scurrying around the

226

house, barking at the doors and nosing a pair of socks she's found behind the sofa around the lounge floor.

I roll my eyes and lean against the door weakly. I should have known it wasn't a good idea to let her join the local amateur dramatics group. But she and Sophie had stormed into the church hall and both expected greatness. Instead, they were both bloody munchkins in the show.

'Good God,' I mutter.

'Woof.' My daughter sits up in front of me and begs, her tongue hanging out and her head tilted to one side appealingly. She has dropped a sock at my feet.

'Isa, I have to go to work. I can't play at being dogs right now,' I tell her. I'm lucky that they've given me back my hours so I don't want to annoy them by rocking up late.

'Woof! Grrrrr.'

'Dear Lord.' I lean down and throw the sock across the floor for her.

'Woof!' She bounds after it.

I grab my handbag off the table and check that Isa's school bag and overnight bag are ready. She's away to Sophie's tonight — it's Friday and they have AmDram after school, then Ruth, Sophie's mum, very kindly offered to take Isa for a sleepover. And she genuinely *is* taking her, because I've spoken to Ruth about it. After the incident of the fire I make damn sure that I know exactly where my daughter is going to be and who with. She knows herself she lost some trust with that one — and yes, I know she was with Scott. It's not as if she was wandering the streets with a litre of cider, but she should have told me.

And Scott should have told me too, instead of believing the word of a ten-year-old. He knows that now. He's been party to a few tantrums — but, amazingly, it hasn't put him off.

'Believe me — she's a proper angel compared to what Nessa was,' he told me one day, and I almost choked on my tea.

Isa tires of her dog act and stands up. 'What are you doing after work?' she asks, her eyes drilling into mine.

I feel the heat creep into my cheeks. I know fine well what I'll end up doing, but I have to keep it clean. 'I'm seeing Scott. As you know.' It still feels a bit weird referring to him as 'dad', as in, 'I'm seeing your dad'.

Isa pulls a face. 'He said he'd teach me some more Black Sabbath. He mentioned Rainbow and Anthrax as well.'

I keep my face studiously blank at Anthrax. 'And he will,' I tell her. 'Next time you're there.'

'Which will be tomorrow. Won't it?' she asks, with a challenge in her eyes. It must be a little difficult for her — she has this sense of possession over me, and now she has a sense of ownership over Scott too. She doesn't want to feel she's missing out on anything, but neither does she want to give up her own pastimes and amusements.

'Yes.'

'Good.' She nods decisively and picks up her overnight bag. I know there's a teddy bear in there, but she would never admit it. He goes all over with her. He's always in the bag for when we stay at Scott's, which is practically every weekend now. The cow-jug has already moved in, and he lives on the windowsill of her bedroom there, which is anything but girly and pretty — but it's what she wants.

I have a feeling she'll be a goth girl or a biker chick when she grows up. She's awfully fond of the motorbike and polished it voluntarily last weekend.

Isa slings her school bag over her shoulder and walks into the hallway. She stares back at me, as if it's me that's been delaying things, not *her* delaying things by being Toto.

'If you don't want to go to drama,' I say, knowing I have to offer — just in case she really, really doesn't want to be a munchkin — 'you don't have to.'

I hope she doesn't see me cross my fingers behind my back.

'No. It's okay. I'll go.' She sighs theatrically and tosses her glorious red hair back. She's refused to put it in a ponytail or anything today. Only Nessa can make her tie it back or wear ribbons, which has given me an even greater sense of respect for Scott's sister. 'After all, *someone* has to show Sophie how to be a munchkin properly.'

I bite my lip to hide my smile and nod. 'Absolutely. Come on, now. Let's go.'

And I finally manage to shoo her out of the flat.

I'm just locking up behind me when my phone goes. It's Scott.

'Liza — I'm really sorry. Can you just let yourself in tonight? I've got something going on.' He sounds odd, and to be fair it is still quite early so what the heck can he have going on that he knows will take all day? Having said that, he has been saying something about a 'Big Project', so I can only assume it's part of that.

'Is it part of your Big Project?' I smile

into the phone. He's making it sound all mysterious and high-risk and I'd love to know what it is.

'Aye. The Big Project.' There's an answering smile in his voice and my knees go a little weak.

'Mum!' Isa shrieks at me from the gate. 'You tell me *I'll* be late, then when Dad rings, you're all kissy kissy, mmmmm, I love you, I love you, I *love* you.' She turns her back to me and mimics arms wrapping around and cuddling her by folding her own arms as tightly around her body as she can and wiggling her hands. I flush to the roots of my hair.

I turn my own back on her. 'Okay. Look, I have to go as Isa is being a demon, but that's not a problem about tonight.' I grin and lower my voice. 'Shall I run the bath for you coming in?'

'Will there be something special in it?' he teases.

I flush even redder. 'Maybe.'

'Maybe you?'

'Maybe me?'

He chuckles and I'm surprised I'm still upright, to be honest . . .

'Mum!'

'God. Right. Okay. I'm going. I'll see you later.'

'See you later.' There's a beat and I hear the rush of water and a rustling and an earthy sort of snapping noise, like he's stood on a twig or something. 'I love you, Liza.'

'I love you too. I — '

' — MUM!'

Okay. Clearly, I *am* going. Time and tide and Isabels wait for no-one.

But I'm damn well looking forward to bathtime.

# 20

## Scott

I've had a couple of weeks to work on things — on my Big Project, no less — and I've hated keeping things from Liza, but needs must when the Devil drives — or so they say.

Or when I drive.

Whatever.

Anyway, I'm lurking on the corner of the street where the vet's is, and I'm chewing the corner of my nail. I'm not entirely sure if this is going to be a good thing or not. I'm waiting for Liza to finish her shift and she's not expecting me, so I'll have to hope she gets out on time or I'm going to look a total fool standing here.

But that problem, at least, is negated, because she comes out with a tall, slim blonde girl and they're laughing together. This must be Magda — she looks Eastern European and Liza has told me about her. Still, I lurk in the shadows, not quite knowing if she wants me introduced to everyone yet.

But some sixth sense makes Liza look my way and her smile widens even more. She taps Magda on the arm and points to me. 'This is Scott. What a lovely surprise!'

'Ooh, Scott.' Magda flashes a grin at me. 'I have heard all about you, yes? You and Leeza. And Isa, the little girl.' Magda nods at Liza. 'He is a keeper. I like 'em dark as well. You have good taste.'

I'm not sure what to make of that, but I smile back. Liza laughs and says her farewells to Magda.

'Sorry,' she says sneaking into my embrace.

'No worries,' I say. 'Do *you* like 'em dark?' I pull her towards me, even closer.

'The darker the better,' she murmurs, and I smile into her hair.

'That's good to hear. But I'm afraid I've taken a bit of a liberty, so I hope you still like me after this. You know my Big Project? Well — this is what it was.' I take a deep breath. 'I think I've found a place you can use for a new antiques shop.'

She stiffens and I swear inwardly. This was wrong, so wrong —

'Your Big Project? It was *that*? Oh Scott! I don't know. I don't know if I'm ready to try again. After all, I'm only entitled to half that insurance money and that means half the size of the shop I had. No — sorry — half the size of the *floor* of the shop I had.' She pulls away and she looks terrified. 'I don't think I could go through it all again. What if it's just not meant to be? Oh God, I'm so sorry your Big Project was that and you've wasted your time . . . '

I put my fingers under her chin and tilt her face upwards. 'I haven't wasted my time. Not at all. What if it *is* meant to be? What if Phoenix Antiques was only a way to get us together? What if this new place *is* for you? What if it means that you can spend more time on it, now you've got me to help with Isa?' I look at the vet's behind us. 'You might even be able to leave hairless rodents behind at some point.'

As I speak the words, I realise I've never really thought about it like that, but maybe it could be true. Nessa is always going on about Fate and what's meant to be will be, *yada yada yada*. It's entirely possible that's what happened. That's what *had* to happen before we could reach this point.

I try again. 'Anyway, you've got *all* the insurance money. You've got mine as well.'

'You can't give me that!' she cries.

'Yes, I can. You gave me Isa,' I tell her simply. 'It's all for her benefit, anyway.'

'I don't know what to say.' She shakes her head and her brown eyes fill with tears. I really didn't want to make her cry, and I feel so guilty I kiss them away as they spill down her face.

'Look — just come with me. Let's

see what you think. Mr Hogarth has just had this place come up — it's perfect. Or at least I think it's perfect. Perfect for you.'

'Mr Hogarth?' She laughs a little bit through her tears. 'I might have guessed.'

'Don't even ask. Just don't ask.' I furrow my brow, contemplating it.

'Is he really just a private detective? He's like some sort of property mogul.'

'Exactly my thoughts. Nessa keeps her information very close to her chest. She says it's safest after the shih-poo incident.'

'The what?'

I shake my head. 'Never mind. It's a dog thing. Now — are you coming to have a look or what? The thing is, I was originally going to do it up and have it all ready for you, but I decided to rein myself in, so I didn't in the end. I didn't know if you'd want it, or whether it would be worth my while. So, I just did one or two things which can easily be undone — '

'No, I'd love to see it!' She smiles and it's like the sun has come out. She lays one hand, palm flat, against my chest. 'Are we going on the bike?'

I grin. Liza loves the bike. I'm pleased I brought the bike here instead of the van.

'Yes, we are. Come on.' I take hold of her hand, kiss it and lead her to our chariot.

## Liza

I hang on, riding pillion, the world a comfortingly muffled sound beyond my helmet. Scott drives carefully through some pretty tree-lined streets, and ends up in the Old Town, the Water of Leith rushing by us, the water cascading down from the Pentland Hills, hurtling beneath St Bernard's Well and along towards Dean Bridge.

He pulls up outside an immaculate, stone-built terrace, near a grand-looking residential area. 'This is it,' he says.

I clamber off the bike and look around me. The area is quiet enough to be nice and high-end, but close enough to the city to be popular with tourists. Despite myself, my heart starts thumping. I can see where this is going already.

Right next to us, one of the terraced houses has been converted into a shop front. I have a feeling it's going to be one of those deceiving places where you walk in, and it's enormous.

'I've got the key here. Do you want to go in?'

He's standing there looking sweetly embarrassed, his helmet clutched before him like a shield. I don't think I've ever seen him look quite so thrown, and it's lovely, in a way.

'Yes. I'd love to,' I tell him, and hold my hand out. He drops the key into it, and it feels warm in my palm. He takes my helmet from me and melts a little into the background, which is something he's quite adept at doing when he wants to. I think he feels this is something I have to do for myself.

I step towards the building and unlock the door. It swings open smoothly and I'm right — it's huge. I'm standing in what was clearly a hallway when it was really a house, and there is a corniced arch before me. To the left is a big room with a fireplace, surrounded by original plasterwork, and a room to the right echoes that. Ahead of me, through the hallway, are two more rooms off to the sides, and the hallway stretches further back again.

'There's a couple of rooms upstairs as well,' Scott says from behind me. 'With a kitchen area and a tea-shop bit, already done out. And you've got a tea-garden as well — a bit bigger than our old courtyard, with a beautiful view over the river and a walk down to the water. I think you can see the Well if you hang over the railings. A perfect place for a *cuachag*, I think.'

I turn to look at him and I'm speechless. The light breaking in through the stained glass semi-circle above the door spatters the black and white tiles with colour and touches Scott like a halo. The rooms are decorated in a beautiful Wedgewood blue and the plaster and ceilings are bright white.

'Did you do any of this decorating?' I manage to ask him, but he shakes his head and his fringe flops around, so for once I can see both his eyes clearly.

'Nope. It was all done. I did some work in the garden. Do you want to have a look? The stuff I did is easy to dismantle, like I said. I didn't want to go overboard with the interior, just in case you didn't like it.'

'It seems perfect,' I say carefully and reach my hand out to him, almost as if I want to draw him towards me for solidity and reality, because this very much feels like a dream.

'But? I sense a 'but' after that comment,' he says, quirking a smile.

'But I don't think I could afford the lease. And where are you going to work if I do?'

He shrugs. 'Out of my stable. Like

always. I've got my van. I can take stuff around in that if people want to see anything.'

'But you want a display room for your samples and everything — you'll want to use this place too.'

'Only if there's a little corner you don't want to use. And you *can* afford it. Mr Hogarth is a very generous man.' He shrugs again. 'Nessa says he despises nepotism, but I do think the price he's quoted for here is very reasonable. It's less than it was at Phoenix. He's using his part of the landlord's insurance for the fire to even it up — or something. I don't know. I just pretended to look intelligent and nodded a lot when Nessa explained it.'

I know for a fact he's lying. Scott has run his own business, very successfully, for years. He knows exactly what the arrangements are, but I think I'll have that conversation with him another time.

For now I'll just focus on this

beautiful place. 'Can we go outside?' I ask.

'We can,' he says, and he moves past me, tossing our helmets onto the bottom of the grand staircase, still holding my hand, so he's leading me out through the back of the premises, through the French doors and into the garden.

There's a wee balcony out of the French doors and a set of well-worn stone steps going down into the wide, grassy expanse of garden. To one side of a flagged path is a swing set, and I grin, recognising it as the set we had at Phoenix. To the right, there are some wrought iron tables and chairs already set up.

A bit further, and we go down another, smaller set of stone steps into a wilder part of the garden. There are some trees and a walk down towards the river as Scott had promised. Strung through the trees are some lamps, intertwined with fairy lights. I just know on a nighttime they'll glitter and sparkle and light the way for people strolling down there.

I stop and stare around me, and suddenly there's a click. I turn and Scott has leaned over and pushed a hidden switch with his free hand. I see now the lamps are all jam jar ones, just like the ones I'd mentioned to Scott once before.

He waves vaguely at the lights in the leafy canopy above us. 'What do you think?'

I just shake my head, which is difficult to do when it's tipped back so I can stare above me. It's even more difficult when my jaw is hanging open.

'I don't know,' I say, which is a really stupid thing to say — but it's true. I don't think I have the power of words to explain how it feels or what I think.

I bring my head back to its normal level and look at Scott. His eyes are drilling into mine and he takes my other hand and draws me close. He leans down to me in that way that makes my knees weak, and I press closer to him.

'There's a summerhouse as well,' he whispers.

'Is there now?' I ask, my voice shaking, but it's not because I'm overwhelmed by this place — it's because I know exactly what will happen if we walk into that summer-house.

He nods and leans down a bit further, putting his forehead against mine, so our eyes are barely centimetres apart. 'Do you want to see it?' he asks.

'Yes.'

'Are you sure?'

'Yes.'

'It's quite secluded.'

'Good.'

He smiles and kisses me, then pulls away and leads me through the woodland. I can hear the river rushing by and just smell the faint metallic tang of the so-called spa water from St Bernard's mingled with damp leaves and fresh earth.

The summerhouse is sitting at the bottom of the garden, and it's got a little rope around it, with a sign saying *Private* dangling off it.

'Oh look. We can't go in,' I say, teasingly.

'Yes, we can,' he replies and scoops me up, stepping over the fence and striding to the summerhouse, where he shoulders the door open.

There's a sofa and some cushions and a rug, and it's like twilight in there, hidden away from the world. It still smells a little of fresh paint and it's all sage-green and cream inside. There's some bunting strung across the window, but that's all I notice as he stands me on my feet, and we move closer towards the inevitable.

I giggle and he stares at me, his eyebrows raised. 'What's so funny?' he asks, a smile threatening at the corners of his mouth.

'Just thinking. At least when Isa and I move in to your place, and we can't ever get any privacy any more, we'll have this summerhouse. We'll just have to put a padlock on it.'

His smile breaks through and he takes hold of my shoulders. 'Seriously? You're going to move in? Like I keep asking you?'

I nod, feeling reckless. In for a penny, in for a pound.

'And if you think it's not too horrendous living and working together, I'll let you have a corner of my shop to play in,' I say, walking my fingers up to his collar and back down so I can get hold of his T-shirt and his jacket and help him out of them, because I'm nice like that.

'I think I can handle it,' he says and rubs his nose against mine. 'I definitely think I can.'

And then I finally get his jacket and T-shirt off, and he returns the favour, and I don't notice much else for a very long time . . .

# Epilogue

## Three Months Later

### Liza

Isa is squabbling with Sophie upstairs — the noise is drifting through the window into the garden, and I wonder at which point in life the genetic code switches on that makes a pre-teen allergic to sunlight.

It's a glorious day and they would rather be upstairs, in Isa's room, arguing about who is going to go for the lead role in the next drama club production. It's *Annie*, so Isa thinks it's a done-deal for her to portray the feisty red-headed orphan and I don't disagree, on principle.

However, Sophie has a slightly better singing voice, so I wouldn't like to be the one who has to choose between them.

I guess we'll just have to be around to deal with the fall-out in an adult-sort-of fashion, if Isa isn't chosen. At least she can rant about being Sandy the dog this time, instead of Toto.

I leave them to it and head down to our very own swing. In Isa's absence, I'm going to take advantage of it. I settle myself onto it, nursing a mug of tea, pushing myself back and forwards gently using my toes. The afternoon is still warm and quiet enough for me to hear the back door click, and I look up to see Scott saunter down the pathway towards me.

He's been at our not-so-new-now shop, which we ingeniously named Belle and Scamp — yes, Isabel got her plump, white kitten in the end as well as a shop sort of named after them both — to take a delivery. He told me under no circumstances was I to order any more pashminas, and I have to concede he was right. He's been taking a delivery of books, paintings and antiques today — just exactly what I always dreamed of selling. The tea-shop is doing a roaring trade upstairs, and I've got twinkly lights wrapped around the banisters already. Mr Hogarth also, somehow, recommended — via Nessa — a fabulous young lady called Eve to work there, and now it's her domain, more or less. She's been a pastry chef in Paris, and worked somewhere amazing in London, and creates the most mouth-watering treats.

Scott lurks around the building too, and has an incredible knack for appearing out of nowhere and helping customers pick the perfect accessories. I must say, Schubert is prone to lurking as well. He'll sometimes just pop in and greet us, but then sometimes he stays for an hour or so and assists Scott. I was concerned at first, because he's a cat roaming around a big town — but Nessa says he sometimes enjoys a constitutional, and I've stopped myself from worrying about it, as he's always found his way home. But as good as my word, I let Scott have two rooms in the end, not just a corner — and one of the other rooms overlooking the garden is my little club room. I've got a book club and an art club going already, I've got an art exhibition on and more things planned. The tea-garden has been wonderful as well, and Scott's right. A *cuachag* like me loves being by the water, and I always make sure our west-facing windows are inviting because you never know who might pay you a visit.

Apart from Schubert, of course. Who is here in our garden at the minute, suffering in dignified silence as Scamp bounces around him and wants to play. Schubert looks over at me and I swear he's just rolled his eyes, and I smile at him sympathetically. Scott's family warned me it was never a good thing to agree to babysit Schubert, but I haven't had any issues with him yet and the adoration between him and Isabel is apparent for anyone to see. How could I say no?

Then, as if Schubert just gives up on

anything resembling dignity, he flops onto his back and grimaces, as Scamp dots around his head, batting his ears in delight.

Isa's swing, the one I'm currently borrowing, is at the far end of our own garden, next to the sunken trampoline and the treehouse. Isa didn't get her latest wish, which was to create a swimming pool right next to the trampoline so she can bounce off it, straight into the water. Even Scott isn't daft enough to give into her for that one — not in this climate anyway.

The play area is far enough away from the house to give Isa some privacy — she's started to think it's uncool to play on the swing and slide and climbing frame, but I know she still does it. I've heard her singing to herself when I've been in 'my' stable, with my paints and my art equipment and my upcycling junk. The play area is also the perfect place for Scamp to sit and clean his whiskers, which is exactly what he's doing at this very moment, as he's seemingly now bored of taking swipes at Schubert. He's great friends with Schubert, and it is lovely to be honest. Nessa said it was one of her greatest wishes to have a friend for Schubert, so they are both — apparently — delighted with Scamp.

It takes Scott a few moments to reach me, but that gives me a few moments to appreciate the way he walks, the way his black T-shirt clings just where it should, the way he has such an easy grace and elegance about him. I smile and raise a hand in a wave, and he waves back.

'All sorted and not a pashmina in sight. Any room for me on there?' he asks, leaning down as I raise my face to his. Our lips brush as he kisses me. He's still got the power to make my toes curl.

'No.' I shake my head. 'Sorry, this seat's taken.'

'What a shame,' he says and smiles lazily, a mischievous glint in his green eyes. 'I'll just have to go on the trampoline instead. Or tell on you.'

'Tell on me. Dare you,' I respond,

and go so far as to stick my tongue out at him.

He laughs and leans against the oak tree, one of his legs bent behind him, his foot in its black biker boot resting against the trunk. We've got a sensible family car, as well as the van and the motorbike now, but I know Scott went to Belle and Scamp on his bike today.

And even if I didn't know that, I would have guessed it, because he's got that look of exhilaration in his eyes.

'No. I don't think I'll tell on you today,' he responds. 'I think I'll just study the view from here instead. It's kind of nice.' He pushes his hands in his pockets and grins.

'Be my guest.' I smile back, then look down into my tea. It's maybe a good moment to tell him. I can't hide it for much longer. I put the tea-cup carefully down on the ground and look up at him.

I take a deep breath. 'Scott,' I say. 'I'm pregnant. It was the summerhouse day, I think . . . I wasn't sure until now

— I thought it was just the stress of moving and getting the business up and running and — '

But as my words tumble out, suddenly he's no longer by the tree. He's in front of me and he's pulling me to my feet and he's laughing and exclaiming that he can't believe it and it's the best news he's ever had.

And then he kisses me, before pulling away and laying one hand carefully on my just-rounding-off tummy, and he says, 'Hello littlest one!' And then he kisses me again, ever so gently, and I throw my arms around him. I'm laughing and crying both at the same time, and I'm kissing him back.

And I'm happier than I've ever been in my life.

I'm like a phoenix, rising from the flames to greet a new day.

And it feels incredible.

# Thank You

Thank you so much for reading, and hopefully enjoying, Scott and Liza's story — I hope also that everybody who's been waiting anxiously for the next Schubert story appreciated the fact that Fate was right, and those two quite mythological alter-egos were meant to be together, dark fairy-tales not withstanding!

However, authors need to know they are doing the right thing, and keeping our readers happy is a huge part of the job. So it would be wonderful if you could find a moment just to write a quick review on Amazon or one of the other review websites to let me know that you enjoyed the book. Thank you once again, and do feel free to contact me at any time on

Facebook, Twitter, through my website
or through my lovely publishers
Choc Lit.

Thanks again, and much love to you
all,

Kirsty

xx

*Other titles in the*
*Linford Romance Library:*

# KISS ME, KATE

## Wendy Kremer

When Kate Parker begins work as the new secretary at a domestic head hunting company, the last thing she expects is to fall for her boss! Ryan Hayes, who runs the firm with his uncle, is deliciously appealing. But beautiful and elegant Louise seems to have a prior claim to him, and what man could resist her charms? Plus an old flame makes an appearance in Kate's life. Could she and Ryan have a future together — especially after Louise comes out with a shock announcement?